"Don't flinch," he said. "I'm not going to hurt you. Anytime you want me to stop, just tell me."

His fingertips were exploring the clean line of her cheekbone. His touch was infinitely tender, and she felt melting weakness flow through her. The darkness, the soothing softness of his voice and his touch were mesmerizing her. She wanted only to lie here and be lovingly stroked. Lovingly. How had the word suddenly insinuated its way into her consciousness?

"I've wanted to touch you like this since the moment I saw you in the ballroom."

Her chest was so tight she could scarcely breathe. The darkness was heady with the scent of cinnamon and thyme, and the clean, woodsy scent of the man beside her. At last she spoke.

"Was that before or after you decided you might have to shoot me?"

He gave a low chuckle. "It was immediate, and I'm beginning to think it may never change now."

Loving. The word again brushed through her mind with the same delicacy as his touch on her cheek. It was crazy to think of the word in connection with Sandor Karpathan. He was hard and dangerous . . . and loving. And he wanted her. . . .

Bantam Books by Iris Johansen
Ask your bookseller for the titles you have missed.

WHAT ARE *LOVESWEPT* ROMANCES?

They are stories of true romance and touching emotion. We believe those two very important ingredients are constants in our highly sensual and very believable stories in the *LOVESWEPT* line. Our goal is to give you, the reader, stories of consistently high quality that may sometimes make you laugh, sometimes make you cry, but are always fresh and creative and contain many delightful surprises within their pages.

Most romance fans read an enormous number of books. Those they truly love, they keep. Others may be traded with friends and soon forgotten. We hope that each *LOVESWEPT* romance will be a treasure—a "keeper." We will always try to publish

LOVE STORIES YOU'LL NEVER FORGET
BY AUTHORS YOU'LL ALWAYS REMEMBER

The Editors

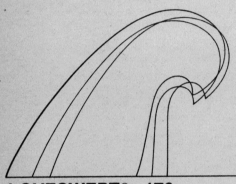

LOVESWEPT® • 176

Iris Johansen
'Til the End of Time

BANTAM BOOKS
TORONTO • NEW YORK • LONDON • SYDNEY • AUCKLAND

TIL THE END OF TIME

A Bantam Book / January 1987

If you would be interested in receiving protective vinyl covers for your Loveswept books, please write to this address for information:

Loveswept
Bantam Books
P.O. Box 985
Hicksville, NY 11802

ISBN 0-553-21794-1

Published simultaneously in the United States and Canada

Bantam Books are published by Bantam Books, Inc. Its trademark, consisting of the words "Bantam Books" and the portrayal of a rooster, is Registered in U.S. Patent and Trademark Office and in other countries. Marca Registrada. Bantam Books, Inc., 666 Fifth Avenue, New York, New York 10103.

PRINTED IN THE UNITED STATES OF AMERICA

O   0 9 8 7 6 5 4 3 2 1

One

"You shouldn't be here," Danilo Jannot said, gazing at Sandor with a disapproving frown. He quickly closed the door and turned the lock. "I could have handled everything here in Belajo. Safeguarding the Ballard woman isn't worth the risk of your getting captured. If Naldona got his hands on you, we'd be in a helluva mess."

"Not for long. You know very well he wouldn't be able to resist the pleasure of sticking my distinguished head on a pike in the town square." Sandor Karpathan's dark blue eyes twinkled. "Then our army would have a martyr, which might be even more beneficial than having a leader."

"Don't joke. You know what your capture would do to our cause. You're the spearhead of the revolution, the savior of Tamrovia, the Tanzar. Without you, the revolution would vanish like a pricked balloon."

"Dear Lord, I hope not." Sandor wearily rubbed

the back of his neck. "If that's true, a good many men have died for nothing, and I've wasted two years of my life. One man can't embody a successful revolution. Why do you think I've trained Jasper and Conal?"

Jannot shook his head. "Jasper and Conal are good men, but they aren't the Tanzar." He looked intently at Sandor. "You are tired. Have you eaten?"

Had he eaten? Sandor couldn't remember. It had been such a long day—but all his days were long now. "I ate this morning," he said at last. "At least I think I did."

"And it is almost midnight now." Jannot looked at him sighing with affectionate exasperation. "Sit down. I will get you something and we will talk. This foolish business of not taking care of yourself must stop." He turned and bustled toward the door to the kitchen at the rear of the small café. "Keep the lights turned out. I'll leave the kitchen door open, and it should give you enough light to eat your meal. The patrol comes by once or twice a night, and we wouldn't want someone to glance in the window and see you sitting here. Naldona has posted pictures of you all over the city. There's no question you would be recognized."

As Jannot disappeared into the kitchen, Sandor dropped into a chair. He leaned his head against the wall and closed his eyes. He had no desire to turn on any lights. The dimness was a soothing balm on his taut nerves, and there were few occasions when he could wrap himself in silence and solitude these days.

Tanzar. How the hell had he become a hero? He'd never made any effort to appear anything but what he was—a man who was willing to fight for his beliefs. Now his people were identifying him with the revolution itself and forgetting others who had been just as responsible as he for bringing their forces to this point of near victory. The thought sent a chill down his back. He wasn't a superman. What if he were killed? They were too close to their goal now to lose everything because one man died.

Sandor opened his eyes to see Jannot setting a plate and a tankard before him on the red-and-white-checked tablecloth.

"It's only a sandwich, but there's some fine smoked ham I managed to hide from Naldona's scavengers when you laid siege to the city. I will be glad to see you put an end to this war. I dislike serving my customers this scanty fare."

"You make it sound so easy," Sandor said dryly. "As if all I have to do is lift a finger and Naldona's defenses will crumble away. If he manages to get Bruner's help, it could extend the war another six months." He took a bite of his sandwich and found that, in fact, he was very hungry. "And that mustn't happen. I will *not* have more men die because Naldona won't admit defeat." His tone was one of cold ferocity. "I'll kill him myself before I'll let that happen."

"Do you think we wouldn't have taken care of it for you if it had been possible?" Jannot sounded faintly reproachful. "His personal security is impregnable. Otherwise I would have given my informant in the palace that small duty. He would have been delighted. His cousin was tortured and murdered by Naldona's goon squad. We can't touch Naldona."

But they would have tried, even though they

knew it would be almost certain death, Sandor thought. Jannot and his men of the underground resistance forces here in Belajo had displayed a courage in the past two years that would have earned them a chestful of medals if they'd been in the field. "I know you would," he said gently. He lifted the tankard to his lips. "But it won't be necessary if we can stall Bruner from making a move until Zack Damon gets the munitions to us that we need for the final assault." The beer tasted cold and biting as it slid down his throat. How long had it been since he'd had anything but field rations? "And we *will* stall him. It's only a question of how to go about it. Fill me in on the details. Your messenger only gave me the bare bones of the story."

Jannot shrugged. "The bare bones is all we have. James Bruner, the American munitions manufacturer, is here at the palace with his mistress, Alessandra Ballard. Naldona is wining and dining Bruner to try to persuade him to ship the weapons he needs without cash up front. Obviously, Bruner has been stalling since the leak to the Human Rights Commission regarding Naldona's treatment of prisoners."

Zack and Kira Damon had spent weeks before the Commission displaying the evidence Sandor had managed to smuggle out of Tamrovia. He would have to remember to send a message to let them know their efforts had not been in vain. Kira needed that knowledge. Sandor knew how painful it had been for her to stand on the sidelines these past years instead of entering directly into the fray. "And the Ballard woman has enough influence to sway Bruner?"

Jannot nodded. "So Fontaine says. They're not demonstrative in public, but do appear to be very close. He calls her his private secretary, but there's little doubt she's his mistress. They occupy the same suite at the palace and she travels with him constantly."

"It's possible a secretary would do that." Sandor smiled. "Sometimes things aren't always what they seem. What makes Fontaine so sure?"

"The woman herself."

Sandor lifted a brow. "Sexy?"

"According to Fontaine, the lady has a body built for one delightful purpose. Bruner would have to be a fool to occupy a suite with her and fail to take advantage of that purpose. And Bruner is no fool. She's been with him a long time, which would serve to strengthen the bond. Yes, Naldona has a weapon he can use."

"And intends to use." Sandor finished the sandwich and leaned back in his chair. "When?"

"Tomorrow night. We're not sure how, or what the exact circumstances are, but Fontaine says the woman will definitely be murdered and the crime laid at your door."

"Which would infuriate Bruner and motivate him to step over into Naldona's camp to get revenge." He gave a low whistle. "A plan worthy of a Borgia. He might have been able to pull it off if Fontaine hadn't tumbled to the plot."

"Go back to your base," Jannot said. "Let us handle this. Your place is with your men."

"My place is where I want to be." There was the sudden sharpness of steel in Sandor's voice. "And I want to be here, Jannot."

Jannot's eyes widened. It had been a long time

since Sandor had spoken to him in such a fashion. He had been allowed to forget who Sandor Karpathan was, but now he had been abruptly reminded. Sandor might be younger than Jannot's own grandson, but he was man enough to have become a legend to his army and the people of Tamrovia. "What do you wish me to do? You know I meant no disrespect . . . sir."

Sandor muttered a curse beneath his breath. "Damn, I'm sorry, Danilo. I'm a little on edge." His hand tightened on the handle of the tankard. "I thought all we had to do was wait. We're so *close*." He drew a deep breath. "It will work out. I'll make it work. All we have to do is stop Naldona from harming the woman and keep her safe until our own arms shipment arrives."

"Not an easy task. There are all sorts of ways he can get to her at the palace. Poison, knives, bullets."

"Then, we'll have to get her out of the palace. That's why I'm here. None of your men knows the palace as well as I do. I spent over a year there before King Stefan was deposed, and I became familiar with every nook and cranny of the place." His lips tightened grimly. "I made it my business to be sure I did, after I began to suspect Naldona wasn't the republican I originally thought he was."

Jannot had forgotten Sandor had been personal adviser to King Stefan during the tension-fraught period preceding the revolution. It was difficult to connect Sandor Karpathan, the Duke of Limtana, with Sandor Karpathan, the *Tanzar*. Yet perhaps the latter couldn't have existed without the former. Sandor's inborn arrogance, his charisma, had made him a remarkable leader. He was a brilliant man, who handled those from all walks of life with finesse. "He fooled all of us. Don't blame yourself."

"Whom else should I blame? I helped Naldona overthrow the monarchy," Sandor said wearily. "I didn't realize he was a Marxist, until it was too late. Men have died because I made that mistake." He finished the beer in two swallows and set the tankard down on the table. "The deaths have to stop. Naldona isn't going to get his hands on Bruner's weapons."

"You'll need our help to get you into the palace."

"Perhaps not. Who is occupying Princess Kira's former suite?"

Jannot blinked in surprise. "I believe that's where they've put Bruner and his mistress. It was the only suite with two bedrooms, and Naldona thought Bruner would prefer to maintain the private-secretary fiction."

"Well, that's a stroke of luck, anyway." Sandor rose to his feet and stretched lazily. "But since you don't know when the murder of the woman is to take place, I'll have to do a little investigating before I can devise a plan. What happens tomorrow evening?"

"A large cocktail party at seven, followed by a small dinner party. It will be attended by all Naldona's loyal sycophants." He frowned. "You're not planning on going to . . . Sandor, it would be suicide!"

Sandor shook his head. "I'm afraid you're right. I may have to use Fontaine. I'll decide after I've taken the Ballard woman's measure." He clapped his hand on Jannot's shoulder. "But that's tomorrow. Tonight, old friend, I'd give my soul for a bath and a clean, soft bed. I can't remember when I last had either."

"Use the bathroom in my quarters. They're in the rear of the café, the first door on the left after you enter the kitchen. I think I can find clean clothes in your size. I try to keep a large stock on hand." His lips tightened bitterly. "When we're occasionally able to liberate prisoners from Naldona's cells, their clothing is almost as torn as their bodies."

"But thanks to you and your men, we've been able to mend quite a few of those bodies," Sandor said gently. "Remember that, Jannot." His smile suddenly lit his face with warmth.

It was the first time tonight Jannot had been exposed to the charm that was an integral element of Karpathan's character. The strength of the man's personal magnetism always came as a shock to Jannot, even after all the years he had known him. No wonder he held sway over Tamrovia with no visible effort on his part. The diplomat and nobleman had evolved into the *Tanzar*. And the *Tanzar* must be protected at all costs. "I would offer my bed as well, but it's not safe for you. I have a bed in the cellar where you can sleep. There's a trapdoor down there leading to a fruit cellar with a concealed exit to the shop next door. I'll feel better if you sleep there."

"Whatever you say." Sandor stood up, stretched again, and walked toward the kitchen, stopping just outside the pool of light that shone through the doorway. "Get in touch with Fontaine and tell him I want him here tomorrow morning. I have a few questions to ask him." He paused in the doorway, his long, lean body framed in silhouette against the light issuing from the kitchen. "Once I get the woman out of the palace, she won't be able to remain in Belajo."

"I'm already working on a way of smuggling her out of the city." Jannot shook his head. "But I'll have to double the precautions if you're going to be with her. You'd be a much bigger fish than Alessandra Ballard for the patrols to net."

"I made it through the barricade tonight in the usual way."

"We won't chance it. Leave the matter to me." Jannot picked up the plate and tankard from the table. "You tend to your business and I'll tend to mine. That's how we've managed to get this far. Go to bed, Sandor." He glanced back over his shoulder with a slightly sardonic smile. "With all due respect, Your Grace."

Sandor made a sound that was half snort and half growl. "You give me about as much respect as that thorn in my side, Paulo Debuk."

"How is Paulo?"

"Paulo never changes. We all have to make adjustments to accommodate him."

"I'm surprised he let you come to Belajo without him."

"He's on reconnaissance in the hills." Sandor lifted his hand. "Good night, Danilo. And thank you."

"You can thank me by being careful tomorrow night." Jannot growled. "We can't lose you now, Sandor."

"You won't lose me. I enjoy living too much to risk opting out of the human race." He shook his head wearily. "Or I will when this damned war is over. I'll see you in the morning, Danilo."

The tall, graceful silhouette of the man vanished from the doorway.

Alessandra Ballard leaned forward toward the mirror to brush a dusting of powder over her nose. She didn't know why she bothered. It would be shiny again in a few minutes. Her skin always glowed with the depressingly bucolic ripeness of a peach. "I'll be ready in a moment," she said over her shoulder to the tuxedo-clad man standing in the doorway of her bedroom. "I'm sorry to keep you waiting. I was late getting back to the palace."

"Did you have a successful afternoon?" James Bruner strolled into the room and dropped onto the Queen Anne chair. "Lord, I hope so." He leaned his neatly barbered gray head against the high-cushioned back of the chair and regarded her with mock reproach. "This is the third day in a row you've left me to fight off Naldona's persuasions by myself. I'm too old to enjoy this marathon of verbal fencing."

She grinned at his reflection in the mirror. "The hell you are. You know you take great delight in stringing our pompous dictator along. Besides, I certainly couldn't have helped you with him. He slots all women in the same category as his teen-age mistress." She made a face. "And Lord knows she's no mental giant."

He shrugged. "Perhaps. However, Naldona is getting a bit desperate. I have an idea Karpathan is pushing him to the edge. I think it's time we left Tamrovia."

She nodded as she scooted the stool away from the vanity table, then rose. "I'll need one more day. I've contacted a priest who will act as administrator, but I still have to discuss the details of the distribution network and bypass procedure."

He smiled as he stood. "You always make your projects sound like a very complicated heart operation."

"They are complicated." She crossed the room and linked her arm with his. "And a heart operation isn't a bad simile, either, is it, James?"

"No." He patted her hand. "Whatever you do always has plenty of heart, Alessandra." His gray eyes softened in affection. "I guess I can stall Naldona for one more day. But no longer."

"No longer," she agreed. She wrinkled her nose. "Now I guess we'd better put in an appearance at that blasted cocktail party. Am I presentable?"

He frowned. "Barely. The gown you're wearing must be five years old. We'll have to stop in Paris on our way home and do some shopping."

"If we have time," she said with a grin. "I don't know why you insist on trying to make me into a lady of fashion, James. I'd think by now you'd realize what a rough diamond you've acquired."

"Just hardheaded, I guess."

"You'll have to accept the fact you've polished this particular diamond to its highest luster and leave it at that." Her smile softened to gentleness. "You have to remember what raw material you were given to work with."

His expression of mocking amusement faded to be replaced by pain. "I do remember. I'll always remember, Alessandra."

She felt a swift surge of remorse. Dammit, she should have chosen her words more carefully. She knew the burden of guilt James carried every day of his life. She quickly lowered her lashes to veil her eyes. "Perhaps I will let you buy me a new gown. I wouldn't want you to be ashamed of me in Mariba."

"Mariba?" Surprise replaced the pain in James's face. "Where the hell is Mariba?"

"It's the capital of an island in the Caribbean called Castellano. I've done some research, and I think that most likely it will be our next stop. The government there is on a par with Naldona's regime as far as oppression is concerned."

He chuckled and slowly shook his head. "You're always one step ahead of me. Do you suppose we could go home for a few days first, so I can see if I still have a factory?"

The shadow was gone from his face, thank heavens. "I don't see why not. I believe I can fit it into our schedule." Her long lashes lifted to reveal dark eyes dancing with mischief. "Provided we skip our visit to Dior and St. Laurent."

James chuckled, and he suddenly looked a good decade younger than his sixty-seven years. "We'll discuss it."

"Of course we will. Haven't I always been a reasonable woman?"

"When your determination doesn't get in the way," James said dryly. "Then reason doesn't stand a chance." He glanced at his wristwatch. "You're right, we'd better get going. It's almost seven-thirty, and we wouldn't want to make Naldona impatient. He's going to be difficult enough to handle without a fit of temper to contend with."

She fell into step with him as they left the bedroom and crossed the sitting room toward the door leading to the hall. "Those fanatical eyes of

Naldona's remind me of that picture of Lenin on display all over the Kremlin."

"His eyes aren't the only thing about him reminiscent of Lenin. His politics fit quite nicely into a Bolshevik niche." James frowned. "I'll be glad as hell to get away from here. Tamrovia may have a certain Balkan charm, but when it gets down to basics, civil war is a dirty business whether it's in Tamrovia or Guatemala." He stopped, his expression clouding again. He added in a tone just above a whisper, "Or Said Ababa."

Her hand tightened on his arm. "But we're not in Said Ababa now. That's finished. In the past." Her gaze held his with compulsive force. "And what happened there is finished too. There are only places like Tamrovia and Mariba and what we can do here and now." She drew a deep breath and deliberately loosened her tense grip on his sleeve. "And what we can do at the moment is smile and be perfectly charming to Marc Naldona." She suited action to her words and fixed a brilliant smile on her lips. "Shall we do that, James?"

He touched her cheek with an affectionate forefinger. "Yes, we'll do that." He grimaced as he opened the door. "After you, my dear."

Alessandra found her smile becoming increasingly strained as she circulated among the guests in the ballroom. She was never comfortable in this kind of atmosphere, though she had trained herself to appear at ease. She always felt as if she were drowning in perfume and smoke and the crosscurrents existing beneath the small talk floating on the surface of the party. Lord, when were they going in to dinner? At least at the table she'd only have to be polite to her immediate neighbors.

"Miss Ballard, may I speak to you for a moment?"

She broke off in mid-sentence to glance at the young man at her elbow. She had to concentrate for a moment before she could place the rather nondescript face. Michael Fontaine, one of Naldona's minor aides. "Yes, of course." She excused herself from the portly businessman to whom she had been speaking and followed Fontaine a few paces away, to the bar against the wall.

He handed her a fluted glass from a tray on the bar and smiled at her with a charm that made his plain face appear handsome. "I thought you might be thirsty. Our guests have been keeping you so busy, you haven't had a chance to touch the drink you were served earlier."

She studied him thoughtfully as she accepted the glass. "You must have been watching me closely to notice that. Why would you—" She broke off as she felt a piece of folded paper pressed against her palm as he transferred the glass into her hand.

He met her startled gaze. "Read it," he said softly. There were lines of tension about his lips as he shifted his position to form a barrier between her and the rest of the guests in the room. "Quickly."

She hesitated as she searched his face. It was more than tension. Fear. He was frightened. She put the cocktail glass down on the bar and swiftly unfolded the small note. It was very brief and scrawled in bold black script.

Come to me on the terrace. If you don't come, you will quite probably die. Mention this note to Naldona, and the man who gave it to you will most certainly die. K.

Alessandra slowly crushed the note in her palm. "K.?"

Fontaine moistened his lips with his tongue. "There are some names that aren't safe to mention here."

Karpathan? She felt a tingle of shock run through her, and her gaze went involuntarily to the French doors. The most wanted man in the country was only a few yards away. Practically in Naldona's grasp.

Her gaze shifted across the room to the small, elegantly clad man speaking with burning intensity to James. It wasn't only Fontaine who would die if she mentioned the note. The man who had written it would have no chance either. She reached for her cocktail and sipped it slowly. "The phrasing in the note could be interpreted as a threat, you know."

"No threat. A warning."

"Interesting." Her gaze moved to the French doors again. "He must be quite a man to inspire you to take a risk like this. You must trust his judgment a great deal."

"He's been watching you this evening and thinks you will not betray us," Fontaine added simply. "And he is the Tanzar."

Tanzar. "Does that mean he walks on water?"

He shook his head. "Loosely translated, it means the man who gives all. But when the people refer to Karpathan, it means something more. The man who *is* all."

"I see." She didn't really, yet she was undoubtedly intrigued. She had no use for politics or folk heros, but she had a sudden desire to meet this Tanzar and hear what he had to say. She put the glass back on the bar. "Can you cover for me if I slip out?"

An expression of profound relief appeared on his face. "With no difficulty. I've gained considerable practice in the art in the last two years. Drift over to the terrace doors. I've arranged for Naldona to be summoned to the study for a phone call. He'll be kept busy for fifteen minutes. I'll watch the doors and make sure no one goes out on the terrace while you're there."

"You have it all planned." She turned toward the door. "Just make sure James isn't worried about me while I'm gone."

"I'll take care of it."

She began to wander casually in the general direction of the French doors leading to the terrace.

Sandor hadn't expected her to be tall. Jannot's terse description had brought to mind the image of a Bardot-type sex kitten, but there was nothing kittenish about the woman slowly making her way toward the terrace doors. Alessandra Ballard was close to six feet tall, built on queenly lines, and every inch radiated voluptuous earthiness. The aura of lushness she projected filtered through the sheer Austrian drapes of the French door and reached him clear and vibrant as a siren's call. No wonder Fontaine had been sure she was Bruner's mistress. Though she was probably twenty-seven or -eight and Bruner rapidly approaching seventy, Sandor doubted that even Methuselah would have been immune to her sexuality.

There was certainly no question of his own arousal, he realized half incredulously. His body had responded the moment he had seen her, and now he felt it hardening to near-painful readiness as she walked toward him. Hell, what was wrong with him? It hadn't been that long since he'd had a woman, and Alessandra Ballard couldn't even be termed pretty. Her shining nut-brown hair was worn in a severely simple bun on the top of her head. Her features were definitely irregular. Large, wide-set dark eyes glowed serenely beneath winged brows. Her nose was a trifle long, and her lips were a little too full. However, her neck and shoulders were truly magnificent, and the sight of the full globes of her breasts springing from the low-cut square neckline of her white gown made a simmering heat start to tingle through him.

He stepped back into the shadows as she opened the door and stepped out on the terrace. She closed the door behind her.

"Karpathan?" Her voice was a mere thread of sound, but clear and unafraid. Her eyes, searching the shadows beside the door, were also free of fear. "Let me see you. You've obviously been out here watching me. It's my turn now."

His surprise was instantly replaced by amusement. He stepped out of the shadows into the moonlight. "Miss Ballard." He bowed mockingly. "I assure you it wasn't my intention to deprive you of your feminine rights. I'm afraid it was an instinctive act of self-preservation to cling to concealment. Shall I revolve like a runway model to make amends?"

"That won't be necessary. I can see you quite well now."

Perhaps more than she wanted to see, she thought suddenly. She was experiencing an unaccountable tension that had nothing to do with fear. She could feel it in the contracting of the muscles of her stomach and the tightness of her chest. She had seen newspaper photographs of Sandor Karpathan and knew he was good-looking, but now she saw he was more than handsome. The perfection of his classic features and the crispness of his dark hair were overshadowed by the force field of strength surrounding him. He was wearing a dark sport jacket over a long-sleeved dark shirt and close-fitting trousers, and his tall, sinewy body looked hard and fit.

Hard. Why was she so conscious of the unflinching masculinity of the man? She was suddenly excruciatingly sensitive to the soft fullness of her own body—the swell of her breasts against the chiffon of her gown, the teasing brush of the material against her thighs as the gentle summer breeze pressed the skirt against her body. She drew a deep breath and ignored the urge to scurry into the shadows from which she had called him. The instinct for self-preservation, he had said. She knew that particular instinct well enough to recognize it when she felt it, and it was here throbbing between them. "May I ask why I'm honored by your attention?" With an effort she managed to keep her tone light and slightly mocking. "When I received the note, I wasn't sure if it was a threat or a warning. Fontaine said it was a warning."

Karpathan nodded as he took a step closer. "We haven't much time, so I'll be as brief as possible. Naldona is planning to murder you and lay the crime at my door. He thinks the desire for revenge will push Bruner into giving him the arms he needs."

She inhaled sharply. She was shocked, though she had no reason to be. She had known what Naldona was from the instant she met him. "When?"

There was a flicker of admiration in Karpathan's face. "You're taking this very calmly. No shocked exclamations, no arguments. Aren't you afraid?"

She made an impatient gesture with one hand. "Of course I'm afraid. Why shouldn't I be? But being afraid won't keep me from getting murdered. There's a chance that knowledge might. When?"

"We're not sure. Tonight sometime. I doubt if it will be before you've retired for the evening, but I can't be sure. Fontaine will keep an eye on you at the dinner party. I'll come to your suite later tonight and take you out of the palace." He paused before adding with a touch of sarcasm, "Do you think you can discourage Bruner from occupying your bed for one night? It's going to be difficult enough for me to get you out of here without worrying about stumbling over your aging lover."

"You won't have to worry about stumbling over anyone." Her eyes were fixed on the formal rose garden beyond the stone balustrade. "Thank you for the warning, but I won't need your help. I'll take care of it."

"The hell you will!" He was staring at her in stunned disbelief. "We're talking about a skilled assassin. Do you think Bruner is capable of saving you from Naldona?"

She lifted her chin. "I wouldn't ask him to. It would be stupid to tell James about this. He'd feel he'd have to protect me, and probably get himself killed. James doesn't know how to handle violence."

His eyes narrowed on her face. "And you do?"

"I hate violence, but I know how to deal with it." She started to turn away. "I'd better go back inside."

"Wait just a minute."

His hands were on her bare shoulders. Heat. His hands were only mildly warm, yet she felt a throbbing hotness flowing, spreading, from the flesh beneath his hands to every part of her body.

His face was taut, his eyes blazing, as he gazed down at her. "I'm not about to be dismissed. In case you've forgotten, I'm involved in Naldona's plot. If you die, this war may go on for another six months. I'll be damned if I'll let you send me away with a polite thank you."

"James and I will be leaving the day after tomorrow." To her surprise she found herself trying to placate him. "Now that I've been warned, I'll surely be able to avoid any danger until then."

"Will you?" He gave her a shake that wasn't exactly gentle. "And how do you think you'll do that? Do you know how many ways there are to kill a person? Well, I do. I've become an expert on the subject in the last few years."

The fresh scent of soap and a woodsy fragrance reminding her vaguely of burning leaves clung to his body. She shook her head as much to rid herself of this new sensual impact as in rejection. "Let me go. We're talking about my life. No one tells me what to do with it." Their eyes were almost level as she glared at him. "Damn you, take your hands off me."

He glared back at her for a moment before his hands reluctantly released her. He muttered a shocking expletive before he stepped back. "This isn't the end of it. Until Bruner leaves Tamrovia, your continued good health is very much my concern. There's no way I'm going to let Naldona murder you because you're too stubborn to accept help."

She turned away. "Go back to your war, Karpathan. I refuse to involve myself in the games you and Naldona play with other people's lives."

"Games!" She could hear the roughened sound of his breathing behind her, and it sent an involuntary thrill of fear through her. She felt as if she'd turned her back on an enraged puma. "War is no game, Miss Ballard."

"Isn't it? Perhaps not to the victims, who act as pawns in your political quarrels. I'm afraid your romantic, folk-hero image doesn't impress me any more than Naldona's 'man of the people.' In your own way you're just as ruthless as he is."

"I know." The words were softly menacing. "However, I didn't realize you were aware of that aspect of my character."

Perhaps it had been a mistake to antagonize him by pointing out that she knew how ruthless he could be. She was usually more diplomatic, but her physical response to him had caught her off guard, and she had reacted with instinctive defensiveness. But it was too late now to worry about regrets. She squared her shoulders as she reached for the knob of the door. "I'm fully aware of it. You even put Fontaine in danger to deliver your message tonight. If you'd been wrong in your gauging of my reaction, he very well could have been killed. You knew that and did it anyway." She glanced over her shoulder and met his eyes challengingly. "What would you have done if you'd seen me take your message across the room to Naldona?"

He returned her gaze unflinchingly. "I would have shot you," he said simply. "I had my pistol trained on you from the minute Fontaine approached you. You would have been dead before you opened your lips."

"You would have murdered me?" she whispered. "Shot me down in cold blood?"

"I wouldn't have wanted to do it. It would have come down to a question of choices." His voice was suddenly weary. "If you had spoken to Naldona, Fontaine would have died and Naldona still would have found a way to asassinate you. If you'd died without revealing his complicity, there would have been only one death. I've had to make a number of unpleasant choices in the last two years. This would have been just one more."

And these decisions had left their mark on him. He looked both disillusioned and soul-sick. For a fleeting instant she felt a surge of sympathy, before she recognized the emotion and quickly crushed it. Good Lord, the man had said he would have shot her and she was feeling sorry for him. "You wouldn't have to make choices like that if you weren't set on becoming the great revolutionary hero."

"You're wrong. I have to make these choices now because I made the wrong choice two years ago. It's my hair shirt." His lips twisted. "And I have an idea you're going to be a hair shirt, too, Miss Ballard."

He didn't wait for a reply. He turned and crossed the terrace, fading once more into the shadows.

Alessandra drew a long, quivering breath and closed her eyes for a moment. Then she opened them, smiled determinedly, and opened the French door. Fontaine was standing at discreet attention beside it. She nodded politely, and her smile took on added brilliance as she quietly slipped back into the ballroom.

Two

Lord, it was difficult to sit here and wait. Alessandra leaned back in the Queen Anne chair and tried to relax her tense muscles. She couldn't have been sitting here in the darkness as long as it seemed, or she would have turned into a doddering old lady. Her lips curved in an involuntary smile as she imagined the reaction of her would-be attacker if he crept into her bedroom and found himself confronting the stereotypical spunky old lady.

Then the smile faded as she glanced critically at the bed across the room. Perhaps she should rumple the covers a little more. The dummy she had made with pillows looked realistic enough in the dimness, but a little disarray might—

The door was opening!

The turning of the knob was so quiet, she wouldn't have been able to detect it if her senses hadn't been finely tuned by the adrenaline flowing through her. The muscles in her stomach tautened painfully with fear and anticipation as she silently rose to her feet. It had been a long time. She had forgotten how frightening this moment before the final commitment could be. Her hands nervously clutched the braided cord she had taken from the silk drapes at the window, as she moved to a position behind the door when it began slowly to swing open.

Her heart was beating terribly hard. Could he hear it? Oh, Lord, what a crazy thing to wonder at a time like this. The weirdest thoughts always occurred to her when she—

He was in the room, a small, dark shadow only a few feet away, his eyes on the lump beneath the silken coverlet of the bed. Only one man. Evidently Naldona had thought a single individual sufficient to murder a helpless, sleeping woman, she thought grimly.

Something was gleaming in his hand. A knife. She had always hated the idea of a knife wound, the thin, cold blade piercing her flesh. He was hesitating. There was always a final hesitation before commitment, and evidently her assassin hadn't experienced it before he opened the door. She waited. His reaction would be slower once his mind was settled on his objective. He took a step forward. Now!

The braided cord slipped around his throat as she leaped forward. She used all her strength to tighten the cord, and heard a low gurgle as the man's breathing was stopped. His arms flailing wildly, his hands tore futilely at the cord. Oh, Lord, the hand holding the knife was rising to his throat. One slice of the cord and he'd be free! Her knee quickly buried itself in the middle of his spine as she jerked him backward. She had to end it swiftly. She held the cord taut with one hand and reached for the vase she had set on the edge of the chest by the door. The vase crashed down on the dark head. Shards of pottery flew in all directions, and the man gave a low groan. His knees buckled as he lost consciousness. She released the cord while he fell to the floor.

Alessandra stepped back, her breath coming in little gasps. It was over. She felt her muscles go limp with relief and sudden weakness. She hadn't realized just how frightened she'd been, until it—

"Very good."

She whirled to face the man lounging casually in the doorway.

"Easy." Karpathan held up his hands. "I'm no threat, at the moment." She saw the flash of his teeth in the shadowy darkness of his face. "Actually, after witnessing how efficiently you downed our friend, here, I'm not so sure you couldn't have handled me equally well."

"What are you doing here?" Adrenaline was surging through her veins from the shock he had given her, but she forced herself to appear calm. "You seem to wander over the palace at will. You'd think Naldona had handed you a master key."

"Knowledge is always a key. Haven't you found that to be true?" His gaze flickered to the lump beneath the covers. "I take it that's a decoy beneath the covers, and not Bruner?"

She nodded curtly.

"I didn't think you'd risk having anything happen to him. Did he complain when you ousted him from your bed?" He turned on a small lamp.

Smiling faintly, he took a step forward and knelt beside the unconscious man. He lifted the man's eyelid. "I assure you I would have done considerably more than complain. I would have made it totally impossible. How long has it been since you've had a lover under sixty?"

Bewildered, she stared at him. The leashed violence beneath his words caught her off guard. He seemed more concerned with her sexual habits than with the condition of the unconscious man he was examining with such cool detachment.

"That's none of your business, is it?"

"Isn't it?" He released the man's eyelid. "You're quite a lethal lady. I wasn't sure you hadn't eliminated him permanently."

"I'm not as cold-blooded as you. I was only defending myself." She watched Sander take the braided cord and swiftly tied the man's hands behind his back. "But this should allay any apprehension you might have had about my defending myself. You can leave me to my own devices with a clear conscience. Day after tomorrow I'll be out of Tamrovia and you can go back to your little gam—" She broke off as she caught his menacing gaze. She shrugged, and said instead, "Your revolution."

"Naldona's goons won't be taken off guard again. The danger hasn't lessened because you've won the first round." He sat back on his heels. "Look, promise me you'll leave before dawn this morning and I'll remove myself from the scene. Fontaine can provide enough security for that length of time. I doubt if there'll be another attempt on you before then."

She hesitated and then slowly shook her head.

"It's too soon. I have something very important to do before I leave Belajo."

His gaze became speculative. "I suppose you wouldn't care to tell me what that 'something' is?"

She shook her head.

"I didn't think so. I have an idea you're a multi-dimensional woman, Alessandra." His gaze held the faintest touch of mischief as it rested on the full thrust of her breasts beneath the white chiffon of her gown. "And I'm looking forward to familiarizing myself with every aspect of those dimensions." He reached into the pocket of his jacket and pulled out a snub-nosed pistol and pointed it at her. "I tried to avoid this. You're an exceptionally determined woman. It's a quality I admire, but it does get in the way."

She went very still. "Choices again, Karpathan?"

"Not such a traumatic one this time. The gun is equipped with a silencer, and all I have to do is inflict a slight wound to encourage your cooperation."

"Cooperation?"

He nodded. "First you're going to write a note to Bruner explaining the situation and then you're going to accompany me out of the palace and eventually out of Belajo." His expression hardened. "I told you I couldn't allow you to have your own way in this. There's too much at stake."

"You could be bluffing."

He smiled mirthlessly. "Do you think I am?"

No. She didn't think so. She doubted if Karpathan ever made a threat he wasn't prepared to back up with action. "It won't do you any good. I'm not going to submit meekly, you know. I'll escape. You're not going to get away with this, Karpathan."

"Taking into consideration your rather unique personality, you're probably right." His smile was self-mocking. "I may have bitten off more than I can chew."

"You're damn right you have."

"Still, it may give me the time I need." He made a motion with the gun. "We'll be traveling through rough country. Your gown is lovely, but not exactly appropriate. Change your clothes."

Her eyes widened. "In front of you?"

"I'm hardly going to turn my back. I've seen how efficient you can be in a rear attack." He rose to his feet and stood with easy grace. "I realize you're not experienced with younger men, but I assure you we don't go mad with lust at the sight of a naked woman."

He noted her expression of smoldering resentment again. Odd, he thought.

"I didn't think you would," she said acidly. "I'm sure I've nothing new to show you. I was just surprised." She turned and walked to the antique armoire across the room. "Enjoy yourself, Karpathan."

He lifted a brow. "Thank you. I intend to." He dropped into the chair beside the bed. "Terrorizing young women into impromptu stripteases is what this revolution is all about. I can't tell you how I enjoy this aspect of my 'game,' Alessandra."

She had clearly struck a nerve by using that term to describe his cause. He wasn't even bothering to disguise the bitterness in his tone. Good. Perhaps if he found her presence abrasive enough he'd be willing to release her. She quickly pulled out a pair of jeans and a tailored shirt from the armoire. "No striptease. I'm hardly the type. You'll have to be satisfied with speed."

Satisfied. There was nothing in the least satisfied about the way he was feeling at the moment, Sandor thought. He tried to keep his expression inscrutable as he watched her pull the chiffon gown over her head and toss it on the bed. Dear heaven, she had wonderful skin. The lush ripeness of it glowed in the lamplight, and his palms ached to touch her. Hell, that wasn't the only part of his anatomy aching. He unconsciously moistened his lips as his eyes fixed on her high, full breasts, spilling out of the half bra. With an effort he pulled his gaze away, and found it wandering down to her flat stomach, girdled by a lacy garter belt. "Why do you wear one of those?" he asked suddenly. He nodded to the garters she was unfastening. "You impress me as a no-nonsense woman. I would have thought you'd have preferred pantyhose."

She could feel the color rise to her cheeks as she lowered her lashes to veil her eyes. "I like the feeling of freedom it gives me," she said curtly. "I hate to feel confined. Not that it's any of your—"

"Business," he finished for her. "I appear to be trespassing again. Sorry. I was just curious." He was also curious about the blush that had briefly touched her cheeks. For a moment Alessandra's bold confidence had vanished and she'd reminded him of an uncertain young girl. His eyes were suddenly dancing with mischief. "I thoroughly approve, by the way. There's nothing more alluring." His gaze traveled down her long, silken legs. He repeated softly, "Absolutely nothing." He looked up and caught another glimpse of wild rose color on her cheeks.

Her brow knitted in a scowl, and he heard her mutter something definitely suspect beneath her breath. He smothered a smile as he felt a sudden surge of tenderness. The fierce tigress looked more like a cross little girl as she yanked down her stockings and tossed them on the bed with the gown.

She pulled on her jeans and a peach-colored blouse with swift, jerky movements. She closed the first three buttons of the blouse and stuffed the tails carelessly into the waistband of her jeans. Then she thrust her bare feet into white tennis shoes.

Sandor shook his head. "Socks."

She looked up. "What?"

"Put on thick socks. We have a good deal of walking to do once we reach the hills, and you might as well be comfortable."

"Walking?" She repeated the word with horror. She drew herself up to her full, majestic height. "I do *not* walk, Karpathan. Try to force me and you'll find yourself carrying me." Her eyes narrowed to gleaming slits. "And I'm no feather."

"We'll see," he said. "Socks."

Her glance should have shriveled him on the spot. Instead it only provoked an annoyingly enigmatic smile. She turned and went over to the chest and took out a pair of white socks. "Is that all?"

He shook his head. "Your passport and an extra set of clothes." He stood up and strolled over to the armoire. He pulled out a small canvas overnight case and threw it on the bed. "Use this to pack them in. I'll get Jannot to find you something more portable when we get to the café."

"I won't need them. I told you I won't let you hold me. When I leave the country it will be *my* choice. You should understand that, Karpathan. You're very high on choices."

"Pack it anyway," he said, and smiled amicably. He motioned with the gun. "To please me." He watched quietly as she packed the items he'd designated. "Thank you. Now write the note."

She sat down at the vanity and scrawled a few lines on a piece of notepaper. She stood up and handed him the note. "Satisfied?"

He scanned it quickly. "Very reassuring. You obviously didn't want to worry the old boy. Now I think we'd better leave." He glanced at the still-unconscious figure of her attacker. "You must have given him quite a wallop. He's still out."

"I'll be glad to demonstrate." She strode toward the door. "Coming?"

His lips twitched with amusement. The lady knew all the psychological ploys needed to take command of a situation. He was now put in the position of having to hurry to keep up with his captive. "I'm right behind you," he said dryly, "which I'm sure fills you with the greatest pleasure." He caught up with her in the middle of the sitting room as she was heading for the door leading to the hall. He put his hand on her arm. "No, not that way." He nodded to the solid wall of built-in bookshelves across the room. "There. Wait here while I slip this note under Bruner's door."

That took less than a minute, and then he was striding quickly toward the wall he'd indicated.

Alessandra frowned in puzzlement as she slowly followed him across the room and watched as he twisted one of the candelabra on the wall by the bookshelves. The entire wall swiveled open, revealing a dark, narrow opening. "A secret passage?"

"After you." He inclined his head mockingly and stood aside for her to precede him. "It was a fantastic piece of luck you were quartered in Kira's room. I wasn't looking forward to negotiating those corridors and then possibly finding Naldona had set up his quarters here."

"Kira?" She cast him a startled glance. "This was Kira Rubinoff's suite? But then, how did you know about the secret pass—" She broke off. She had seen photographs of the former Princess Kira Rubinoff, who was now the wife of billionaire Zack Damon. Sandor Karpathan possessed more sexual magnetism than any man she had ever met. It was fairly obvious why two such attractive individuals would have been drawn to each other. "Never mind. It's none of my affair."

"You're quite right, and it wasn't mine either." He added emphatically, "Kira is my cousin and my very good friend. When you leave Tamrovia I'll be very displeased if you spread unpleasant gossip regarding this particular entrance to her suite. So displeased, I might decide to follow you and make my displeasure known."

"Really?" For a moment she was tempted to use the weapon he had put in her hands. Then she shrugged and preceded him into the passageway. "Don't worry, Karpathan, I don't play that way. My fight is with you, not with some poor, gullible woman you lured into your bed."

He suddenly chuckled. "Her husband would be

very amused to hear your description of Kira." He twisted a sconce on the stone wall of the passage and the wall swung shut, leaving them in darkness. "No one lures Kira anywhere. She's almost as determined as you."

She was beginning to believe Karpathan could lure any woman into any indiscretion. She was experiencing a wildly sensual response to him herself, and they had been in a constant state of antagonism since the moment they had first met. Even now, in the darkness, she was conscious of the heat emanating from his lean, hard body, and his clean, woodsy scent seemed to be all around her. Though they were standing at least a foot apart, she felt as if he were touching her. The sensation was so strong, she felt a frisson of panic run through her. "It's dark." Her voice sounded breathless, and she steadied it with an effort. "Are we going to stand here all night?"

He was silent a moment, and when he spoke, his voice was harsh. "No."

She detected a movement beside her, and then the slender beam of a penlight pierced the darkness. His expression was grim, and his eyes . . . She looked away hurriedly. She didn't want to know what his eyes were saying. It was too close to what she was feeling. She moistened her lower lip with her tongue. "That's better."

"Is it? I think it's getting worse all the time." He pulled his gaze away and took her elbow. "Come on, there's a flight of stairs just ahead. Then the passage winds past the ballroom and the dungeons and exits in a cave in the woods across from the front gate." He thrust the pistol into his pocket. "My men are waiting there with a car to take us to Jannot's café."

He had mentioned that name before. "Who is this Jannot?"

"Danilo Jannot, head of the underground resistance forces. He's a good man." His hand on her arm was warm and disturbing. "He owns a small café on the outskirts of the city. His network has managed to free a hell of a lot of people from Naldona's prisons." He glanced down at her with a sardonic smile. "He plays our 'game' exceptionally well. With luck he might even be able to get us through the city gates without being shot by the perimeter guards."

"It's not too late. You could still let me go. I promise I'll be nothing but trouble for you." She was experiencing a spiraling sense of panic again. She didn't want to go with him. For the first time in years, her emotions were in a state of chaos. She thought she had gotten to a point where she couldn't be reached, where she was totally in control. Yet Karpathan had managed to topple her defenses with no effort at all. Sex. It had to be only a powerful physical attraction. She grasped and held on tight to the thought. She repeated urgently, "It's not too late."

She was wrong. Sandor had a gut feeling it was very much too late. In the short time he'd been with Alessandra Ballard, she had managed to arouse lust, anger, amusement, and a fierce sense of his need to protect her. He wasn't sure if he would have let her go now even if his original reason for taking her had disappeared. His hand tightened on her arm in unconscious possession. He had given up practically everything he valued in these hellish years. Didn't he deserve something for himself? Whether he did or not, he knew he was going to take it. He stared straight ahead so she wouldn't see the sudden glint of resolution in his eyes. "Your notion of whether or not it's too late is entirely a matter of perspective." He propelled her gently but inexorably forward into the darkness. "Watch your step. These stairs are steep."

"Any trouble?" Danilo Jannot carefully closed the door behind them and turned the lock. His gaze raked over Alessandra. "Miss Ballard? I'm glad to see you're still in good health. I wasn't sure Sandor would be able to rescue you before Naldona—"

"Wait." Sandor held up his hand to stem Jannot's flow of words. "She doesn't regard it as a rescue, Danilo. According to her, it's more in the line of interference." He grinned. "And there wasn't any trouble, because the lady already had Naldona's hit man garroted and unconscious as I appeared on the scene."

Jannot grinned. "Perhaps we should recruit her, eh, Sandor?"

Sandor shook his head. "Miss Ballard prefers Mr. Bruner's 'games' to ours, Jannot. I guess we're going to have to work on changing her mind."

"Miss Ballard is becoming very irritated at being spoken of as if she weren't here." Alessandra pronounced every word with precision. "As well as being abducted and having her life put in danger."

Sandor's eyes twinkled. "You've listed your objections in a rather unusual order of importance. Which do you regard as the most heinous crime?

I assure you I couldn't be more conscious of your physical presence."

Jannot chuckled, and Alessandra felt the heat rise to her cheeks. Dammit, why did everything Karpathan say or do have such an effect on her? She was sure she hadn't blushed in all the years before he'd come into her life.

"She wasn't willing to come with you?" Jannot's smile faded. "Shall I put a guard on her? It's not safe to start you on your way until almost dawn."

"That won't be necessary. I'd hate to put anyone else in the line of fire." He met her gaze. There was something in his eyes at odds with the lightness of his tone. "I feel she's my personal responsibility."

Jannot shrugged. "Whatever you say. You have another five or six hours before I can move you. You'd better take her down to the cellar to wait."

Six hours alone with him in the intimacy of a cellar? "Couldn't I stay up here?" she asked quickly. "I've already been dragged through a secret passage, a dungeon, and a cave tonight. I think I'd prefer to remain topside."

"It's not safe. Not for you, and certainly not for Sandor. He's taken too many risks already for you."

"For *me*?" Her eyes kindled with indignation.

But when she opened her lips, Sandor's voice quickly cut across her protest. "Jannot is right. You'll be safer downstairs." He took her canvas overnight bag and handed it to Jannot. "She'll need a backpack and a slicker."

"I'll see to it." Jannot turned away. "Try to get some sleep. There's no telling how long you will have to stay in the *labone* if Naldona puts on additional guards."

"*Labone?*" Alessandra asked warily.

"It's a Tamrovian word. It means . . ." Sandor's words trailed off, and a slight smile tugged at his lips. "On second thought, I believe I'll let you discover for yourself. I think I'm mired deeply enough in your bad graces at the moment." He gestured for her to precede him. "I promise you won't find Jannot's cellar too unpleasant."

When Sandor pulled the cord of the overhead light in the cellar a few moments later, she was relieved to discover he was right. The small room was devoid of furniture except for the narrow single bed in the alcove formed by the stairs. The walls were lined from floor to ceiling with shelves containing jars filled with everything from horseradish to spices. The cellar was neither damp, cobwebbed, nor rat-infested, and the entire area was scrupulously clean. The concrete floor was scrubbed, and the air, though close, smelled deliciously of the spices that lined the shelves in large, squat jars.

"Surprised?" Sandor asked.

Alessandra nodded. "And relieved. I didn't particularly care for our stroll through the secret passage." She wrinkled her nose distastefully. "A rat ran across my foot when we were going through the dungeon."

"Did it?" His gaze was fixed intently on her face. "Yet you didn't say a word at the time."

She shrugged. "What did you expect me to do? Screaming wouldn't have done any good." A faint twinkle appeared in her eyes. "And I'm too big to leap into your arms for protection. We would have both landed on the floor with the rat."

"So you ignored it." Sandor slowly shook his head. "You're a very unusual woman. I'd give a good deal to know what experiences developed that uniqueness. I don't suppose you'd care to tell me the story of your life?"

"No." She turned away from his probing glance. "You can stand here all night, but I'm going to get some rest. There's no telling what kind of hurdles you're going to put me through once we leave here." She strode across the room in the direction of the bedstead. "I'll take the bed."

"Will you, indeed?" Sandor's lips curved in an amused smile. "Why do I have the feeling you're trying to take charge, Alessandra?"

"I'm always in charge," she said serenely. "At the moment that fact might be obscured, but I assure you it will become clearer as time goes on." She sat down and kicked off her tennis shoes and swung her feet onto the counterpane of the bed. "Good night, Karpathan."

"Sandor." He reached up and jerked the light cord. The cellar was suddenly engulfed in darkness. "I always insist on first names with a lady when I'm sharing her bed. It adds a comfortable note of intimacy."

Alessandra inhaled sharply. She felt as if she'd been kicked in the stomach. She had hoped to avoid this confrontation. Sometimes, if she was aggressive enough, it took the edge off an adversary's own aggressiveness. She should have known it wouldn't work with Sandor Karpathan. "You won't find this bed either comfortable or intimate." She deliberately threaded her tone with fierceness to hide the faint quaver she knew would be there. "And if you touch me, I'll take great pleasure in emasculating you, Karpathan."

He laughed with genuine delight. "Damn, I think you would." He was moving toward her in the darkness. "And if I weren't so tired, I believe I'd accept your challenge, my ravishing Amazon." He paused beside the cot. "But I *am* tired, and I have no intention of napping on the cold concrete floor, when I could be resting beside you. All I'm asking is that you share your bed, not your body. Now, scoot over, Alessandra."

"There's not enough room for both of us."

"Then we'll make room." He sat down, and she had to scurry to the far side of the cot to keep from being sat on. She turned on her side, her back pressing against the wall.

"See? It's amazing what a small amount of space two people can occupy when they try." He stretched out, and she felt the lean, hard muscles of his thigh brush against her leg. It felt warm and solid, and she tried to move closer to the wall to escape him. "Oh, for heaven's sake, I'm not trying to rape you. Relax."

"I don't want to be here. Let me up."

"Don't be stupid." He turned on his side to face her. "Look, I won't promise not to touch you. That would be impossible in a situation like this, but I will promise I won't assault you. You'll find my word is good."

She was silent a moment. She knew Karpathan's word could be trusted. It was as much a part of the legend surrounding him as his brillance in military maneuvers. She forced herself to relax. "Your promise isn't precisely all-encompassing," she said warily. "I think I should ask you to add a clause or two."

He chuckled. "You're as safe as you want to be. Beyond that, I'd be a fool to offer more." He paused. "You are aware of how much I want you, aren't you?"

His words came as a shock. She hadn't expected him to be so frank. "Yes."

"Don't get up-tight about it. I can practically feel you bristle. It's not as if you don't want me too."

"I don't—" She broke off. She *did* want him, and the sensual electricity crackling between them had been too powerful for either of them to ignore. She refused to play the coy, simpering maiden. "Yes, but I'm not going to do anything about it." She paused deliberately. "And neither are you, Karpathan."

"Damn, I love your bluntness." This time his low laugh held a note of curious pride. "And your honesty. I hate people who say one thing and do another. There's going to come a time when we're going to do a hell of a lot about it, Alessandra. No, don't bristle again. I just wanted to be as honest with you as you have been with me."

The man was incredible. "Has it escaped your notice that threatening to shoot a lady doesn't exactly act as an aphrodisiac?"

"I was afraid that was going to be your reaction." He sighed. "I guess we'll just have to be satisfied with exchanging other intimacies for now."

"Other intimacies?"

"Conversation, viewpoints, experiences. Nothing very threatening." His voice lowered to velvet gentleness. "I didn't want to threaten you, Alessandra. My life seems to be constituted of threats and force these days, but not because I want it that way."

She wasn't sure his gentleness wasn't more threatening than the pistol he had pointed at her. She felt a minute melting somewhere within her, and she instantly braced against the breach in her defenses. "I'll try to remember that next time you're forcing me to do something against my wishes," she said caustically. "Unless you've decided to turn over a new leaf and let me go?"

"No, I can't do that." There was sincere regret in the simple statement. "I can't even say I want to let you go. I want you in a position where I can study you."

"Study? You make me feel like an insect under a microscope."

"Hardly an insect, but you're definitely a new species to me." His hand reached out to gently touch her cheek. "Don't jump. I'm not going to hurt you. Anytime you want me to stop, just tell me."

His fingertips were exploring the clean line of her cheekbone. His touch was infinitely tender, and she felt melting weakness again flow through her. The darkness, the soothing softness of his voice and gossamer touch were having a mesmerizing effect on her. She found she wanted only to lie here and be lovingly stroked. Lovingly. How had the word suddenly insinuated its way into her consciousness?

"I've wanted to pet you like this from the moment I saw you in the ballroom."

Her chest was so tight, she was having trouble

forcing breath into her lungs. The darkness was heady with the scent of cinnamon and thyme and the clean, woodsy scent of the man beside her. It took a moment before she was able to force the words out. "Was that before or after you decided you might have to shoot me?"

"Before, during, after. I'm beginning to think it may never change now."

Loving. The word again brushed through her mind with the same delicacy as his touch on her cheek. It was crazy to think of the word in connection with Karpathan. He was hard and dangerous and . . . loving. The word popped up through the haze with maddening persistence. "What are you saying?"

"That you have a very peculiar effect on me." His fingers drifted up to rub her temple with a touch as light as a breeze on a May morning. "I want to know you." His laugh held a note of wonder. "Lord, I've never wanted to know everything about a woman before, but I do now. I want to know what you like and don't like, what you think." His voice abruptly hardened. "And why the hell you have a lover who's more than twice your age." He felt her stiffen against him. "Oh, all right, forget that last, but we'll definitely be going back to it."

"I don't think so." She spoke with a coolness she didn't feel. "Take your hand away, Karpathan."

He removed it instantly, and she immediately experienced a wild sense of loss.

"You see, no threat," he whispered. "But I think you're missing it as much as I am. I believe touching each other may become addictive for us. Now that you've seen how obedient I am to your every wish, may I touch you again?"

She opened her lips to refuse, but somehow the words didn't come. After all, what harm could it do? Being caressed by Karpathan was very pleasant, and, as he had said, there was no threat.

He rightly took her silence for assent and his fingertips were once more stroking her temple. "That's right, relax. You don't have to do anything, not even make a decision. I'll take care of everything."

It had been a long time since there had been no decisions for her to make. She closed her eyes and let the blissful warmth and security flow over her. "Only because I want to rest for a while, Karpathan. I'm still the one who's in charge."

"Of course you are," he murmured. "But it wouldn't hurt to talk to me. That's what darkness like this is for. You can toss out a word or sentence and it just floats away. Talk to me, Alessandra." His fingers were smoothing the soft hair away from her temple. "Are you an American?"

"I have an American passport. What is this, some kind of third degree?"

"Perhaps. How long have you been with Bruner?"

"Since I was fourteen."

His hand hesitated before resuming stroking. "Remind me sometime to tell you what I think about dirty old men." The harshness in his voice was barely controlled. "He obviously wanted to catch you young enough to train you to his specifications."

The roughness of the condemnation jarred her out of her dreamlike state of contentment. "You don't know what you're talking about. James isn't a dirty old man." A sad man, a tormented man, but certainly not lascivious. "And our relationship is none of your concern. I think you'd better let me up. I'll sleep on the floor."

"No." His silence following the protest was charged with conflict. "I won't mention Bruner again. Stay."

"No more questions?"

"Not unless you want to ask them of me."

"Why should I do that? Everyone knows about Karpathan, the Tanzar. The newspapers love you. You're a romantic hero."

"Lord, what hogwash," he said with a growl. "I'm a soldier. Nothing more."

That wasn't true. He was also a man, and she was becoming more conscious of his blatant masculinity every moment. "You're also the Duke of Limtana, playboy, millionaire, Oxford scholar, second cousin to deposed King Stefan. Your mother was Argentinian, and she inherited one of the largest ranches in Argentina. She returned to the pampas after your father died. You inherited a fortune from both your father and your maternal grandfather. The newspaper articles made a big fuss over your idealism in giving up your silver-spoon existence for your people." Her tone became faintly cynical. "But no matter what happens to your revolution, your personal wealth is secure, isn't it? You can indulge yourself in your little adventure and lose nothing."

"There's one thing I might lose that I consider irreplaceable," he said quietly. "My life. That's a high price to risk for adventure to relieve my boredom."

She shrugged. "Some men like to live on the edge of danger. Before the revolution you were fond of mountain climbing and race-car driving."

"You appear to be very well versed about my personal history."

"I researched you very thoroughly before I came to Tamrovia." Then she added quickly, "Not from any personal interest, you understand. I made sure I knew just as much about Naldona."

"Researched," he repeated thoughtfully. "That's a curious word to use. Now, why would James Bruner's mistress be curious enough to 'research' the two opposing sides of a war-torn country she was merely visiting?"

Alessandra was silent.

"It's none of my business. Right?" Exasperation and resignation threaded the words. "You're a very difficult woman, Alessandra Ballard." He suddenly chuckled. "But I've never enjoyed anything that came easy. I haven't climbed a mountain in a long time."

"I may be large, but I'm not sure I like being compared to a mountain."

"You're laughing. I'm relieved. I wasn't sure you had a sense of humor underneath all that fierceness."

"Of course I have a sense of humor." It was ridiculous to feel so indignant. Why should it matter what he thought of her? Yet it did. Good Lord, what was happening to her? She drew a deep breath and tried to block out the effect he was having on her emotions. His sensual effect on her was bad enough, but she was beginning to find she actually *liked* the man. She was discovering qualities of patience, humor, and gentleness she didn't want to acknowledge. He was a man to trust. She had developed an instinct over the years of separating the dross from the gold, and Karpathan was the real thing. The affection and respect she had noticed his men gave him was impossible to ignore. Well, she *would* ignore it. She must ignore it. "I don't want to talk anymore." She closed her eyes determinedly. "I'm going to sleep now."

"I think I'm being dismissed." His tone held only indulgent amusement. "All right, go to sleep. I'll watch over you."

Karpathan would watch over her while she slept. The assurance filled her with warm contentment. After a lifetime of relying on no one but herself, for this brief period she could lower her guard. He was the enemy, but for some unexplainable reason she trusted him. She could feel the tension of years begin to splinter and then dissolve. She would have no trouble rebuilding those defenses later, she assured herself drowsily. "I don't need you to look after me, Karpathan. I can take care of myself." She didn't question the impulse that led her to cuddle closer, even as she murmured, "I don't need anyone to take care of me."

Within a few minutes she had drifted off to sleep. Karpathan carefully shifted his position to slide his arm around her shoulders. Even in sleep she tensed with wariness before relaxing again. Soldiers in the field often developed an alertness that followed them into unconsciousness, and he had been forced to learn it himself. But how and where had the pampered mistress of an industrialist acquired the instinct? She was an enigma.

Moving with caution to avoid alerting those instincts, he slowly brought her close until her cheek was resting on his shoulder. Her hair smelled faintly floral, and he lowered his head to breathe in the scent that clung to her skin. The fragrance was as individual, basic, and full-bodied as Alessandra herself.

He supposed he should try to go to sleep, though the possibility was extremely unlikely. His arousal was responding to the touch and scent of her with aching sharpness. He drew a shuddering breath and then wished he hadn't. The lush, seductive woman scent was going straight from his head to his loins. His lower body moved in a thrusting, yearning movement against her. God, he was hurting. Control. He had to maintain control. By some miracle Alessandra had been persuaded to trust him, and he mustn't betray her. He had an idea she gave her trust with great rarity. His arms tightened around her for a brief moment. Let her go. He knew he had to let her go, but, dammit, he . . . He set his teeth and forced his arms to loosen and then withdraw entirely from around her.

He gazed unseeingly into the darkness. His muscles were stiff and unyielding as he tried to fasten his thoughts on something, anything to keep them away from the woman whose cheek still lay pillowed so trustingly in the hollow of his shoulder.

Three

"A *labone* is a *sewer*? No wonder you told your friend I'd need a raincoat." Alessandra gazed distastefully at the round, gaping mouth of the manhole. "I presume it's damp as hell down there."

Sandor nodded. "Sorry. Belajo is a very old city, and the walls of the sewer system have a tendency to spring leaks." He glanced over his shoulder and grinned. "But you'll be glad to know I've seen only a few rats when I've been down there."

"How very comforting," she said dryly as she edged closer to the manhole. She shivered and drew the folds of the black oilcloth poncho closer to her body. She wasn't sure if the shiver was caused by the thought of going down into the darkness of another unknown labyrinth or from the predawn chill. She should have suspected Karpathan would have an unpleasant surprise for her when he had led her to this alley behind Jannot's café. She didn't like burrowing around beneath the ground, dammit. "I'm going to present you with a formidable bill very soon, Karpathan. I'm definitely going to get you."

"I hope so," he murmured as he watched her negotiate the first rungs of the ladder. "Or vice versa."

She glanced up and had to smother a smile. She was grateful it was still dark and the smile went unnoticed. She wouldn't have wanted him to know of the strangely companionable mood she'd found herself experiencing since he'd wakened her twenty minutes earlier.

After a night spent in his arms, she was having problems convincing herself he was still the enemy. It was really a pity. He would have made a wonderful comrade in the old days. Together they would have run rings around the guards, and he wouldn't have been intolerant of Dimitri, as the others had been. . . .

"There are several inches of water in the sewer. When you reach the bottom rung, step to the left. There's a foot-wide ledge that's usually above the water level. Be careful. I can't risk turning on the flashlight until I'm in the sewer and the cover is back in place."

Usually above the water level? She cast an apprehensive glance downward. The air here in the sewer was moist and heavy and smelled abominable. She thought she could faintly discern the glitter of water just below her, and she shifted uneasily on the ladder. She had no intention of landing in that murky water if she could prevent it. There was no telling what manner of disgusting debris was floating in a sewer. She carefully lowered a foot past the bottom rung of the ladder.

The tip of her shoe touched liquid, and she quickly jerked it back.

"Are you all right?" Karpathan asked.

"Did you ever hear the story about there being alligators in the sewers?"

He laughed with genuine amusement. "Yes, but it's just a myth."

"I'm glad you're so confident." Her foot touched the ledge, and she carefully moved to it from the ladder and pressed back against the damp wall of the sewer. "I wouldn't think of questioning your source. If you're wrong, I don't want to know. I'm on the ledge now."

She cautiously sidled a few feet forward. It was awfully slippery. She wished Karpathan would turn on the flashlight. It was even darker down there than before, now that he'd replaced the manhole cover. She heard his steps echoing on the metal of the ladder, but he was only another dark silhouette in a tube of shadows. Then he was on the ledge, and she breathed a sigh of relief. It was odd how much more secure she felt with Karpathan at her side.

The slender beam of the penlight pierced the darkness. His gaze quietly searched her taut face with concern. "There's nothing down here to hurt you. I never would have brought you with me if there had been."

She knew he wouldn't. In spite of the unpleasantness of her surroundings, she'd been certain Karpathan would never expose her to any real peril if he could prevent it. She smiled crookedly. "There had better not be. I'm not skilled at alligator wrestling. The fist one we run into is all yours."

"Right." His hand was on her elbow, propelling her forward. "I welcome the challenge. We modern men are handicapped by the lack of dragons to fight for our ladies. I guess an alligator would do nicely."

His lady. A warm contentment touched her like the crackling heat of a fire on a crisp winter day. She should resent the possessiveness in the words. Yet she found it difficult to do so when it made her feel so exquisitely treasured. She had the irrational feeling that now that she had experienced this warmth, she would miss it when Karpathan took it away. She must be going soft. She had never missed being cosseted before. "I think I'd enjoy watching the show."

"The question is, which one of us would you be rooting for?" he asked dryly. His hand tightened as she slipped a little on the fungus-coated concrete. "Watch it. I wouldn't want to have to pluck you out of that water. You'd be even more perturbed at me if you came out of here smelling like . . ."

"A sewer," she finished for him. "I think I'm already in that condition. How much farther do we have to go?"

"Another half mile or so. This sewer empties into the Gratani River about a quarter of a mile outside the city. Unfortunately there's a road directly across the river controlled by Naldona's troops. We'll have to wait for the diversion Jannot's arranged before we leave the sewer. That should be in about forty minutes."

"Diversion?"

"A guerrilla attack."

"Quite a diversion just to get me out of the city."

"But very worthwhile. I'm becoming more convinced of that with every passing moment."

She glanced back to see a faint smile on his lips.

"Now all I have to do is to convince you, my dear Amazon."

"You'll never—" She broke off and looked away. No doubt Karpathan would regard the denial she'd been about to make in the same light as the alligator challenge. She wasn't sure she was up to facing that particular kind of challenge at the moment. She closed her lips, her steps unconsciously quickening. "Let's get out of here before this odor becomes embedded in my bones."

She didn't know whether the sound echoing behind her was a chuckle or a reproving cluck. It didn't matter. Whatever his response, she knew it would not be meant unkindly. She had discovered that beneath the hard facade Sandor Karpathan assumed, there lay a surprising gentleness.

"For the love of God, move!" There was no sign of gentleness now on Karpathan's face as he jerked her after him up the incline. "Jannot's men can't keep up the artillery fire much longer without being spotted. We have to get beyond the summit of the hill so they can get the hell out of there."

"I *am* hurrying." She twisted her arm out of his grip. She cast a glance across the river. The attention of Naldona's soldiers was concentrated on the bluff bordering the highway, but that could change at any moment. "Go on. Run. I'm not a doll to be carried. I can keep up with you."

Something warm flickered in his expression before he turned away. "I believe you can. Let's prove it, shall we?" He began to run, keeping as low as he could on the open terrain of the path.

Alessandra followed him, moving with the same speed and caution. The path was steep and went almost straight up. By the time they crested the hill, her breath was coming in labored gasps. Good Lord, she was out of condition. But Karpathan was a little out of breath, too, she noticed with satisfaction. "Were we seen?"

"You would have known it if we were." Sandor's lips twisted. "There would have been bullets whistling over the pretty brown bun on the top of your head. But we should keep on going until we get behind our lines. Do you need a rest?"

She shook her head, too breathless to answer.

There was again that flicker of pride in his face. "It's only across the next hill. Our base is a few hours' hike away, but once we're behind the lines, it will be safe to let you stop for a while." He turned away and began to cover the ground at a half trot, trusting her to keep the pace.

Karpathan's trust filled her with the same strange, fierce happiness as the pride she had seen glimmering in his face. In that moment she could understand why Karpathan was supposed to be able to inspire his followers to perform miraculous feats. She would probably have done a hell of a lot more than stretch her physical resources to the limit to have him look at her again with admiration and pride.

However, her limit of endurance had nearly been reached when Sandor called a halt. There was a bead of moisture running down her back and every breath was causing an agonizingly sharp pain in her side as she collapsed against a huge maple tree and leaned back against the rough bark of its trunk.

"We're safe now."

"How do you know we're behind your lines?" she asked curiously as soon as she could get her breath. "We haven't seen any soldiers."

"That's because they know who I am." Sandor dropped down beside her. "Guerrilla warfare. Naldona's men would have been cut down a hundred yards ago."

"I'm glad your men have good eyesight." She grimaced. "I suppose they would shoot me, too, if I wandered away from you."

"Not after they'd seen you with me." He went still. His eyes narrowed on her face. "Don't even think about it, Alessandra. You might be safe from them, but you wouldn't be safe from me. I'd stop you long before you reached the *labone*."

"I have to think about it." She leaned her head back against the trunk of the tree. "I told you, I have something to do in Belajo. I can't leave until I've finished what I started."

"What the devil is important enough to risk getting killed for?" His tone was roughly impatient. "For heaven's sake, tell me."

She opened her lips and then closed them without speaking. She was tempted to give him the information he demanded, but the trust she was learning was too new. Sandor Karpathan's charisma was forceful enough to persuade an angel to give up its wings. What if she were wrong to give him her trust?

An expression close to pain fleetingly crossed his face. "Very well. I can wait. You'll have to talk to me eventually."

She met his gaze and felt a flutter of panic. He was right. If she stayed with him, there was no question that she'd tell him what he wanted to know. It was only a matter of time. Why, she had been trailing after him as meekly as a blasted camp follower! It was incredible how far they had come since she had walked out on the terrace last night.

"No!" She jumped to her feet. "Dammit, Karpathan, I won't let you manipulate me. You've already mesmerized half of Tamrovia. Just let me alone."

"I can't seem to do that," he said simply. "I've given up trying. I believe you'll reach that point, too, before long."

"The hell I will." She whirled and was running back in the direction from which they had come. She heard a low curse and then the rustle of the brush behind her as he started in pursuit. She flew over the ground, adrenaline lending strength to lungs and muscles she had so recently strained to the point of exhaustion.

"Stop, dammit." His voice was low and intense, close behind her. "Alessandra, this isn't—" He broke off as she had a spurt of speed and pulled a few yards ahead of him. She might make it! The sudden effort to escape had been sheer impulse prompted by panic, but there was no reason why she shouldn't succeed. She was strong, and heaven knew she had endurance. Karpathan wouldn't call for help, because he would be afraid it would trigger his men to hurt her. If she could gain a few more yards . . .

She fell to the ground with a stunning force. He had tackled her, she realized dazedly. Karpathan moved quickly astride her. His powerful hand on her nape pressed her face into the grass. She couldn't breathe! She tried to lift her head, but his grasp wouldn't permit it.

"Stop struggling." His tone was as coolly ruthless as his hand on her neck. "You'll either promise to quit fighting me or I'll keep your face pressed into the dirt until you pass out."

She was close to unconsciousness now. She was fighting wildly for breath, and the darkness was lifting and falling.

"Your word," Karpathan demanded.

Damn him, how did he think she could speak if she couldn't breathe? The thought must have occurred to him, for his grip shifted and she was allowed to turn her head so her cheek was pressed to the ground instead of her mouth and nose. "I promise," she said, gasping.

She was flipped over, and found herself looking up at Karpathan's tense face. He was pale. She was the one who had nearly suffocated. Why was he so pale? Her breasts were lifting and falling as she tried to force air back into her starved lungs. Her gaze blazed at him. "For now, Karpathan."

"*Oh, God!*" The words were wrenched from him. "Why are you making me do this to you?" He lifted the short rain poncho over her head and threw it aside. He placed his hands beneath her breasts, with his thumbs on her breastbone. Startled, her eyes widened in apprehension. Then the tenseness flowed out of her as she realized the action was completely impersonal. He was gently compressing and releasing her diaphragm to help her breathe. "*Tell* me. Let me help you. You know I can't let you go." There was a muscle jerking in his left cheek, and her gaze fastened on it in bemused fascination. "Whatever you have to do in Belajo, I can arrange to have done for you. We can work it out. Trust me."

His hands felt warm and gentle through the cotton of her shirt. His dark blue eyes were also gentle in his tormented face. Her anger was suddenly gone. He had done what he had to do. She probably would have done the same.

"Trust me," he repeated coaxingly. "You won't be sorry, Alessandra."

Lord, she hoped not. Because she knew she *was* going to trust him. The decision brought such a lessening of tension it made her a little dizzy. She hesitated. "There's a priest, Father John Dinot," she said haltingly. "I was to see him today to make final—" She broke off to glare up at him fiercely. "If you betray me, I'll come back and cut your heart out, Karpathan."

"You haven't given me anything to betray yet," he said dryly. "What are you up to with the good father?"

"It's for the children." Her gaze moved to a point beyond his shoulder. "They're the ones who are hurt the most by war. You and Naldona will tear the country apart for your damn principles. I've seen it happen before. And all that's going to be left will be the hunger and the suffering. And the children. The children will survive. They always survive. But someone has to help them."

"And is that what you're doing, Alessandra?" His fingers reached out to tenderly brush a tendril of hair from her temple.

She nodded, still not looking at him. "James supplies the money. I find a distributor, such as

Father Dinot, who has no allegiance to either side, and we channel food and medical supplies through a neutral network. In that way we bypass the government bureaucracies which have a tendency to pocket a hefty percentage of relief funds."

"I see."

There was a raw savagery in the tone that brought her gaze flying back to his face. She inhaled sharply. Hurt. Besides anger, there was hurt in the eyes looking into her own.

"And I suppose you're lumping me with the bureaucrats who would rob those children. My God, what kind of monster do you think I am?"

"I didn't know you. You and Naldona deal in power. Power changes people."

"Enough to turn me into a man who robs children?" His eyes were blazing fiercely. "I'm fighting this war as much for those children as for—" He stopped and drew a deep breath, struggling for control. She had struck him where he was most vulnerable. No one knew better than he how power corrupted. Naldona had become a ruthless dictator after his first sip of the heady vintage. Why should he blame Alessandra for thinking he might do the same if given the opportunity? "What do you want me to do? How can I help you?"

Now there was weariness as well as hurt in his eyes. For some reason she couldn't bear to think she had caused Karpathan to look so utterly world-weary. "I do trust you, Karpathan," she whispered. "I know you wouldn't hurt my children."

"Thank you." The grimness disappeared from his expression as he smiled gently down at her. "I think you've given me one of your rare compliments. I don't believe trust in your fellow man comes easily for you, but I have an idea I still have a long way to go. It wouldn't take more than a flicker of suspicion to have you threaten to cut my heart out again." His hands were still pressing and releasing her diaphragm, though her breathing was now as steady as his own. She really should tell him to stop. But the movement was very . . . pleasant.

"Now, let's set a plan in motion to accomplish our objectives." His brow wrinkled in thought. "I can't risk security by bringing Father Dinot into camp to talk to you. Besides, it would be dangerous for him. The best thing would be to send a courier with your instructions. He can also bring a message back." His gaze searched her face. "If you think you can entrust a confidential message to one of my men."

She nodded slowly. "I imagine you're a good judge of character, Karpathan." She grinned up at him. "And you've recently given me a demonstration of the treatment you mete out when someone displeases you. I doubt if your messenger would risk having your wrath turned in his direction."

"This particular messenger doesn't give a damn about my wrath, but I believe you'll agree he's reliable." His expression became grave. "I'll also have a message sent to Bruner to let him know you're safe. The only promise I'll ask you to make is to cooperate in letting me smuggle you over the border into Switzerland."

"I'm not unreasonable. If you can arrange for me to complete my business with Father Dinot, I'll be glad to leave Tamrovia. I can't say I've had a very pleasant stay here."

"I'm sorry. It's really a wonderful country." His expression was earnest. "I could show you places—"

"Karpathan, I'm afraid it's too late for a travelogue. Now don't you think you could let me get up?"

"Sandor," he prompted softly. "I want to hear you say my name."

"Sand—" She inhaled sharply as she looked up into his eyes. They were communicating something so heated and basic, she felt a tremor run through her.

"Again." His fingers on her rib cage were no longer impersonal, but intimately sensual, as they moved beneath her breasts in a slow, easy rhythm. "I like it. Say it again."

Her throat was so tight, she wasn't sure she could form the word again. She was conscious of a slow, hot, melting sensation in her limbs and at the apex of her thighs. Melting, and yet tingling as if those sensitive places were being lazily stirred by the motion of his fingers. "Sandor," she whispered.

"You have the most magnificent . . ." His hands pushed up gently, throwing her full, ripe breasts into bold prominence. His eyes were fastened with searing hunger on the mounds jutting against the cotton of her shirt. "I can still see you standing in your bedroom with your breasts spilling out of that little scrap of a bra." His fingers pushed her still higher. A shudder went through him. "I thought you'd probably spill out of my palms like that too." His fingertips were gently rubbing and smoothing the sides of her breasts. "I'd like to see them do that. I'd like to have you leaning over me, and be able to open my mouth and—" He broke off and closed his eyes. "I lay there beside you last night and thought how soft you'd be if I unbuttoned your blouse and put my hand on you. I kept telling myself just touching you for a second wouldn't hurt." He opened his eyes, and they were soft and glazed with hunger. "But I knew I wouldn't stop there. I'd have to use my mouth and my—"

"Stop." Alessandra moistened her lips with her tongue. Her breasts felt taut and swollen, as if they would burst through the cloth confining them. She was burning up. Tingling. Even the soles of her feet were tingling. "I'm getting confused. I don't want . . . It's too fast."

"I know." The words were grated from between his teeth. "But it's happening. You know it's happening."

She couldn't lie to him. "Yes."

"Good." A little of the tension drained out of him. "At least you admit I'm not alone in this. It helps to know that. It may even keep me from jumping the gun until you become accustomed to the idea." He added quietly, "I probably wouldn't be this generous with my patience if I didn't know there's an excellent possibility we're being watched by the perimeter guards. I want you very much." His hands reluctantly left her. "I've never before wanted anyone or anything this much in my life."

The expression on her face revealed how troubled she felt. "I can't promise anything. I don't know if—"

"Well, I know," he said as he swung off her and rose to his feet. "But I've asked you to promise enough for one day." He took her hand and pulled her to her feet. "You're an honest woman. When you're ready to commit yourself, you'll come to me and tell me." His expression was suddenly grave. "You *will* belong to me, Alessandra."

She bent and picked up the poncho from the grass. "I don't know whether I will or not. You're a persuasive man, but I don't like ties." She looked up to meet his eyes. "And I think you could be very possessive."

"You're right." His lips twisted in a lopsided smile. "Perhaps if I show you my other sterling qualities you'll be willing to put up with one, minor fault."

"Perhaps." She was feeling warm and breathless again, and she determinedly pulled her gaze away. "Don't you think we should be on our way to your base to send that message to Father Dinot?" She glanced down at the poncho across her arm and wrinkled her nose distastefully. "And if I smell as bad as this raincoat, there's definitely another priority I'll have to attend to after the message has gone out. I hope you have facilities for a bath, Sandor."

"We'll arrange something." He took her arm. "Leave it to me."

She was leaving a great deal to Sandor Karpathan, Alessandra thought as she fell into step with his long-legged stride. It was strange that she wasn't feeling even a faint trace of misgiving. Strange and warm and . . . exciting.

Four

"Ho, Sandor, I was about to come after you. I would think you'd know your way home by this time." The huge, bearded man squatting by the fire rose to his feet with a litheness belying both his size and forty-odd years. His dark eyes wandered appraisingly over Alessandra. "But perhaps you were in no great hurry."

"It's difficult to remember the way home, when we change the location of the base every week or so. I don't have your gypsy instincts, Paulo." A little smile tugged at Sandor's lips. "And a few things happened to delay me."

The large man shrugged. "That instinct has to be bred in the bone. But you have other instincts just as amusing. That's why I stay with you." His white teeth suddenly flashed in his bearded face. "You offer the best hunting in Tamrovia."

"Thank you." Sandor inclined his head in a mocking bow. "We try to please. I have a task that might amuse you right now. Or rather, our guest has a task. Alessandra Ballard, this is Paulo Debuk."

"Now, here is a proper-sized woman." Paulo Debuk's massive paw engulfed her hand. "It's about time you found yourself a woman who isn't a bit of meringue. This one has the substance needed to be the Tanzar's woman." He pumped her hand vigorously. "I'm truly delighted you have come to your senses. She will give you fine, strong sons."

"I will?" Alessandra asked faintly. She wondered if everyone who met Paulo Debuk felt as overwhelmed as she did. If he was one of Sandor's officers, he was very strange one. Instead of the green camouflage fatigues worn by the other soldiers she'd seen as they approached the camp, he was garbed in rough denim trousers tucked into brown suede boots. A dark brown shirt with full flowing sleeves was stretched over his broad shoulders and deep chest. Debuk's full dark beard was flecked with gray, but the dark eyes gazing into her own were as bright as the smile he was bestowing upon her. It was a moment before she could arouse herself from her bemusement. What had he said? Something about . . . She hurriedly pulled her hand away. "No. You misunderstood. I'm here to—"

"Miss Ballard and I have made an arrangement." Sandor's eyes were glinting with amusement. "But unfortunately my progeny aren't part of it. Perhaps we can put in an addendum later to that effect. She has a message for you to deliver in Belajo."

"Delighted," Paulo drawled. "It was getting very

dull waiting around here anyway. I'll be glad to have something to do."

Sandor frowned. "No word from Zack?"

"A radio message last night," Paulo said. "But you're not going to like it. There's been a delay in shipping the arms across the border. It will be another two days before they arrive here at the base."

Sandor murmured a curse half beneath his breath. "I was afraid of that."

"Zack is doing all he can. He knows you're having to twiddle your thumbs until the shipment arrives."

"I know. I know." Sandor turned away with barely concealed impatience. "But there has to be some way he can hurry it up. I'm going to see if I can get through to him." He glanced back over his shoulder at Alessandra. "Give your message to Paulo. He's as close to a disinterested observer as you'll find in Tamrovia." He didn't wait for an answer, but strode hurriedly to a large tent several yards across the glade.

Well, that certainly put her in her place, Alessandra thought. As soon as he was again faced with the problems of his revolution, her attractiveness to him faded into the background.

"He's very worried about the weapons," Paulo said gently. He had been studying her face as she watched Sandor walk away. There was understanding as well as sympathy in those sparkling dark eyes. "The longer the delay, the more chance of death and injuries on both sides. Sandor wants it over."

"I know. When ambition calls . . ."

Paulo shook his head. "You think he's ambitious? What can this war give him that he doesn't have already?"

"Power."

"Sandor?" Paulo threw back his head, and his laughter boomed out. "Do you know what he's most afraid will come out of this war? He is frightened they will insist he become president of the new republic. He is tired of being Tanzar."

"He can always say no."

"He is a man who believes in commitment. Such a man has trouble saying no when there is need." Paulo's lips twisted. "And there is always need for the Tanzar."

Sandor Karpathan would quite probably be the first president of Tamrovia! Why did that idea give her such a sinking feeling in the pit of her stomach? She unconsciously squared her shoulders. "Sandor said you were unbiased. Yet you're in his camp and presumably ready to run his errands."

"I am a gypsy. We stand apart from wars and politics."

"Then why are you with Sandor?"

"I like him. He is a fine hunter." Paulo's eyes twinkled. "Almost as good as I am." He paused. "You're afraid to trust this message with Sandor?"

Was she afraid? Her emotions were in tumult. "I'm not sure." She smiled. "But I believe I can rely on you, Paulo. Do you think you can take a message to someone and bring back an answer by tonight?"

"Of course, unless that person is in a solitary cell in Naldona's high-security prison." A wide grin lit Paulo's face. "Then it might take me until tomorrow morning."

Alessandra chuckled. Paulo was obviously larger than life in terms of more than his size. "Don't worry—this person is quite accesssible. That's one of the reasons I chose him."

"Pity. I was hoping for more of a challenge to break the monotony. Do you need a pen and paper?"

She nodded. "Please."

Thirty minutes later she had finished writing the final instructions to Father Dinot and given the message as well as directions to Paulo. She stood watching him move silently through the forest as he left the camp, and slowly shook her head. The man was a giant, a flamboyant giant to boot, and the last person she would have chosen for an undercover mission.

"You look skeptical."

Sandor, frowning, stood beside her. Evidently the radio call had not gone as he wished, she realized.

"Don't tell me you don't trust Paulo either."

She pursed her lips in a soundless whistle. He really was in a bad mood. "I wasn't questioning his integrity, merely his size. Is it safe to send him into an occupied city, where he'll stick out like a sore thumb?"

The frown faded slightly. "He'll be safer than any man I've got. Paulo can come and go in seemingly impossible situations. I think he must take on the protective coloration of his surroundings."

"Amazing," she murmured.

"He'd be the first to agree with you." He took her arm. "Come."

She glanced up at him, startled. "Where are we going?"

"You wanted a bath." He was propelling her toward the perimeter of the camp. "You're going to get one."

"Here?" She glanced around. She could see at least twenty soldiers milling around the glade. "I think I'd prefer a little more privacy."

"It will be private. You've forgotten how possessive I am. I've given orders that anyone within fifty yards of your 'bathtub' will answer to me." He smiled grimly. "In my present mood I think I might be glad if one of them disobeyed."

There was precious little chance his wish might come true, she thought. The aura of leashed violence surrounding Sandor would discourage any trespassers.

Her "bathtub" turned out to be a small, clear pond about a half mile from the camp. It was surrounded by thick shrubbery, forming a nautral protective barrier to guard her privacy.

Sandor reached into his pocket, brought out a bar of soap, and handed it to her. "Don't lose it in the water. Soap is as scarce as all our other supplies right now. I'll go back to the base and scavenge a bit to find you a clean towel, and I'll bring your backpack at the same time." He turned away. "I'll be back in twenty minutes."

She slowly shook her head as she watched him walk away without a backward glance. Just when she thought she had begun to know the man, he showed her a new and different side of his character. She might as well have been one of the bushes rimming the pond, for all the personal concern she'd detected in his parting words. Telling herself he must be upset by the news he had learned didn't lessen her pique. Pique. What a petty emotion. She believed she had outgrown such childish emotions . . . but now it seemed Sandor was inspiring all sorts of feelings to emerge in her—and not all of them pleasant.

Perhaps, she thought, his actions hadn't been as abrupt and impersonal as they seemed. Her past experiences had precluded the possibility of her having much modesty remaining in her make-up, but he couldn't know that. Gallantly, he was providing privacy for her, as he hadn't been able to do last night at the palace. She felt a stirring of tenderness for Sandor, and a slight smile curved her lips as she began to unbutton her blouse.

She was singing. No, it was more of a throaty hum, with an occasional word here and there. Sandor paused before the screen of shrubbery to listen. Lord, there wasn't a more sensual sound on earth than a woman softly crooning to herself. He felt an equally natural and obvious bodily reaction to the unconscious sensuality of the sound. So obvious, he was forced to wait for a moment before pushing his way through the shrubbery.

Alessandra was standing in the middle of the pool, her back to him, her wet hair clinging to her neck and falling in long strands down her back. He hadn't realized her hair was so long. It came to the middle of her naked back, now that it was no longer bound in a bun. Naked. The realization caught him with brutal force. He had been expecting it, yet the shock was still there, tightening the muscles of his stomach and thighs, stroking his arousal with feather-light fingers of electricity. He couldn't breathe. He wanted to look away, hoping some of the ache would disappear if he could no longer see her. Yet he couldn't shift his eyes away from her.

The water in which she stood was waist deep, but clear so that he could see the pale gleam of her lush hips and strong, well-shaped legs. Crystal drops of water beaded her shoulders and the long, beautiful line of her spine. Her skin glowed with a nearly palpable sheen in the dappled sunlight filtering through the trees. He watched in fascination as a small drop of water began to glide with excruciating slowness from her shoulder blade down her back. He smothered a groan as intense desire stabbed his loins.

The low croon broke off, and he saw the muscles of her back tense. "Sandor?"

"Turn around." His voice was hoarse. "I want to see you."

"I don't think—" She stopped. She could feel his gaze on her naked back, and it was sending shivers of sensation through her. Heat. Touching her breasts, burrowing between her thighs. She closed her eyes. She had been about to protest, but she had sensed that this was coming. It was another step forward in their relationship. A step she wanted to take. "I want you to see me."

She turned to face him. She threw back her head proudly, watching his face as he looked at her. Her large breasts were firm and ripe, and she was not ashamed of either their size or the response she knew would be obvious to him. She didn't have to look down to know how swollen or taut she was or how her nipples were jutting out in hard, pointed invitation. She could see it in his eyes as they fastened on her with raw intensity. She inhaled sharply, the muscles of her belly flinching as if from a balled fist.

"Come here," he said thickly, not taking his gaze from her breasts. He dropped to the ground the knapsack and towel he was carrying. To free his hands for her, she thought with a flare of excitement mingled with panic. "Please," he added.

She began to walk toward him. The water was cool and heavy as it ran over her thighs and buttocks. She felt only heat. She was burning up. Sandor was burning too. She could see the flush darken the tan of his cheeks, and his eyes . . . His hand reached out and pulled her from the water to the bank. She felt a sudden shyness pierce her former serenity. "You're very polite," she said with an attempt at lightness. "Do you always say please when you want something?"

He didn't raise his gaze from the full invitation of her breasts. "I'll say anything you want to hear, if you'll let me keep looking at you." His words came jerkily. "And I'll do anything you want me to do, if you'll let me touch you." He slowly bent his head. "Will you let me touch you, Alessandra?"

She couldn't answer. Her throat tightened and then closed entirely when his tongue licked delicately at a drop of water beading the pink crest of her breast. Her body gave its own response, and she heard him laugh with husky delight before his lips closed on her nipple. She moaned, the bar of soap dropping to the ground as her hands fluttered up to tangle in his hair. His mouth was moving with hot, moist urgency, suckling, nibbling at the long, pointed nipple. His fingers were toying with and encircling the swollen spheres as if he were starved for the taste and texture of her. She made a low sound deep in her throat and her fingers threaded through his hair, clutching at him with mindless urgency. Her body was trembling, and she could scarcely stand up.

He lifted his head, and his eyes were dark and oddly blind-looking. "You're shivering," he muttered. "Let me dry you." He bent down to pick up the towel he had dropped to the ground. "Are you cold?"

"No, far from it."

He carefully dried her throat and shoulders. The terry of the towel was gently abrasive against her skin. She tensed as the towel brushed against the exquisitely sensitive tips of her breasts. Sandor's gaze lifted swiftly at the small betrayal, and he smiled.

"Good," he said softly. "Still, I think we'd better get you dry." His hands cupped her breast from below and lifted it into high prominence. The towel moved over the mound slowly and thoroughly, until her breath was coming in little gasps and her gaze was clinging to his face as if she were drowning. "Aren't they lovely?" he asked softly. "Like luscious ripe apples." He lifted the other breast and began to towel it with the same thoroughness. "I feel like I'm shining an apple for the teacher." He gently released her breast and began to dry her abdomen. "Only, I'm the teacher who's going to enjoy them." He dropped to his knees in front of her. "Spread your legs, love."

She obeyed slowly, gazing down at him in bemusement. Her hands were still wound in his hair, and she found herself moving them in a loving, stroking motion. His lips were pressed against her belly, and his tongue suddenly darted out to lick teasingly at her navel. He rubbed the towel up and down on her soft inner thighs with soothing gentleness.

"I like your hands on me." She could barely hear the words, muffled against her skin. "I'd like them all over me. Gentle and then harder, your nails digging into me." The towel was suddenly between her legs. Her hands tightened in his hair as her hips tilted instinctively forward. The motion of the towel was no longer slow and gentle. It was hard and fast, and the rough friction was unbelievably erotic.

"Sandor." The name was gasped between her clenched teeth. "Stop, it's too—"

"Too much?" The towel was instantly gone from between her thighs. Instead it was draped around her buttocks. "I'll try to be more gentle. I'm barely holding on, and it's difficult to . . . " The words trailed off as he began to cover her lower belly with tiny nipping kisses, his teeth pressing just enough to arouse without hurting. He began to move the towel from side to side in a slow, rhythmic tempo. "Is that better?"

If by "better," he meant sheer sensual torture, it was definitely better. The combination of the friction of the towel on her buttocks and the abrasion of his teeth and tongue was driving her insane. "No. I'm *hurting.* I want . . ."

He looked up. His gaze was intent and wild in his taut face. "Are you?" He suddenly dropped the towel, and his bare hands were on her buttocks, his face buried against her stomach as he desperately clutched her close. "Lord, so am I, love." His open mouth was moving over her in a hundred frantic kisses. "I have to be inside you."

"Here?" It wasn't an objection. She was far beyond the point of objection. She only wanted him to make love to her.

His hands clenched her buttocks as he went tense. "I'm behaving like an animal. Is that what you mean?"

Startled, she said, "No, never."

"Maybe I am an animal." His hands released her and he was suddenly on his feet, unbuttoning his shirt. "There have been moments lately when I've wondered if I'd ever be anything else after this damn war is over." He was taking off his shirt and throwing it aside. His fingers were on his belt. "I was ready to throw you down on the ground and take you like one of the whores who follow my troops." He was naked now, and she caught a glimpse of lean, tanned muscles and an arousal so bold, her eyes widened in surprise. "And if you don't get the hell out of here, I'm still going to do it. I won't be able to stop myself." He stepped from the bank and into the pond. Water splashed everywhere as he began to cleave through the pond, his arms moving with explosive violence. He stopped in the center of the pool to look back at her. He stood up, and the water lapped around his hips. "What are you waiting for? Get dressed and get back to camp."

Puzzled, she stared at him. "What's wrong?" She was still aching with an emptiness it now appeared he had no intention of filling. "I wasn't fighting you. I *wanted* you to make love to me."

"I know you did." He scowled. "Will you please put your clothes on? This cold water isn't helping as much as I hoped it would."

"All right." She bent down to unfasten the knapsack, her attention on his bewildering reversal. She pulled out a pair of bikini panties and slipped them on. "You wanted it too." She fastened her bra and thrust her arms into the yellow blouse. "Why did you stop?"

"Because I'm not an animal." His gaze was following her fingers with fascination as she buttoned the blouse. "Yet. And because I don't want to give you a quick roll in the hay you'll be able to dismiss later. When we come together it's going to mean something to both of us. I can wait."

Well, she wasn't sure she could. She stepped into her jeans and pulled them up. She hadn't expected her sexuality to explode this way. It must have been like a ticking bomb inside her all these years, waiting for a spark to set it off. Except Sandor Karpathan was more like a forest fire than a spark, she thought. She could feel his fire touching her still as she stood looking at him. She could feel her breasts swell and thrust against the cotton of her bra as her gaze went over him.

He had looked slender when he was dressed. Naked, his sinewy muscularity belied his slenderness. His broad shoulders tapered down to slim hips and a flat belly. His chest was corded with heavy muscles and feathered with a triangle of dark hair. The thick nest of hair below his belly was also dark, and she found her gaze following in fascination the arrow of springy hair until it disappeared beneath the water.

"Alessandra."

Her gaze flew guiltily up to his face. There were amusement, gentleness, and exasperation in his expression. "Don't do this to me, love. Let me set the pace. All right?"

She hurriedly thrust her feet into her shoes and gathered her discarded clothes together. "My hair's a mess. Do you have a brush I can use?"

"In my tent. Ask anyone to show you where it is."

"Very well. I'll send someone back with a fresh change of clothes for you." She picked up the soap from the grass. "Catch." She tossed him the soap.

He caught it easily, his gaze fixed on her face. "Are you angry?"

"No." She turned away. "But I don't like to have decisions taken out of my hands. You might find our next encounter ends quite differently."

"Lord, I certainly hope so." His voice was so rueful, she had to smile. "A defeat would have been welcome in this particular engagement."

"I'm glad you're resigned to it." She started toward the path leading back to camp.

"Alessandra."

She looked back at him over her shoulder.

"I'm not going to be someone you can walk away from." His eyes were grave. "We want each other, and I'm going to build on that. By the time we become lovers, you're going to be as wild for me as I am for you." He smiled gently. "And then we're going to take the next step."

The next step? She was half afraid to ask what he meant. She'd been bombarded by too many new emotions and ideas already today. She started to turn away again and then stopped. She didn't look at him, and her voice was low. "You shouldn't worry, Sandor. You're not an animal. I know about animals, and you'll never come close to being one." She thrust the branches of the bushes aside and quickened her footsteps toward the path a few yards ahead.

Paulo Debuk didn't return to camp until late that evening. He came as silently as he had gone. One moment Alessandra was sitting alone, gazing into the fire, and the next he was squatting beside her, presenting the note in his hand with a little flourish. "Mission accomplished." He grinned. "I would have been back before sundown, but your Father Dinot had a few errands for me to run. He said he wanted to be able to tell you the lines of communication were in place." He lifted a shaggy brow. "You aren't a spy, by any chance? If you are, I must show you some tricks to move around freely without being seen. People our size must take certain precautions."

"I'm not a spy," she assured him solemnly, her eyes twinkling. "However, if I ever change my vocation I'll know whom to come to for lessons." She nodded at the note in her hand. "You're obviously a very talented man."

"Yes, I am." He reached for a stick and idly poked the fire. "I'm convinced Sandor couldn't have won this war without me."

"Won? You speak as if victory were already a fact."

"It is. That's why Sandor is on edge. It was easier for him when all his energy was centered on winning. He's not good at waiting." He glanced around. "Where is Sandor?"

Her gaze shifted back to the fire. "I'm not sure. I haven't spoken to him since this afternoon. I did see him go into the command tent earlier this evening with several of his officers."

He stood up. "Then I think I will go find him and tell him what a magnificent job I did for you. Not that he will expect anything else. I always do a magnificent job."

"I'm sure you do." She began to unfold the note and looked up to smile at him. "Thank you for doing it magnificently again this time. It means a great deal to me."

"It was nothing." He turned away. "Even if you weren't the Tanzar's woman, I would have done it. It posed a few interesting problems."

"I told you, I'm not the Tanzar's wom—"

He wasn't listening. He was strolling away in the direction of the command tent. His demeanor was casual, almost careless, but she noticed there was not even the snapping of a twig under his foot to signal his departure.

She glanced down at the note in her hand. Father Dinot had been very thorough and gone into great detail. He had listed names, addresses, and personal backgrounds of the people he had chosen as contacts and distributors. She settled down and began to read, her brow furrowed in concentration.

"Satisfied?"

She looked up to see Sandor standing beside her. He had changed into a dark green field uniform and combat boots. The military garb reinforced the impression of toughness and strength he gave. "I think so." She began to refold the note. "I'll have to send someone back to Tamrovia to be sure there's no breakdown in the network, but Father Dinot appears to have made excellent choices."

"Good." He sat down beside her. "I don't suppose you'd give me the information and let me check on it for you?"

She hesitated. "I can't do that."

"I see." A flicker of pain crossed his face. "Your confidence in me doesn't go very deep, does it?"

Her eyes were troubled. "It's the children. I don't have a right to risk their welfare." She met his gaze directly. "I trust what you are today. It's what you may become tomorrow that I have qualms about. I've seen too much. . . ." She lifted her shoulders in a half shrug. "If you can't accept it, I'll understand."

"That's very kind of you." There was a touch of bitterness in his voice. "I don't accept it. I *won't* accept it. It's not good enough. One of these days you're going to tell me you'll not only trust me tomorrow, but for the next fifty years." He stood up and pulled her to her feet. "Come on, let's get some sleep. We have to leave at dawn."

"We? You're going with me?"

"We have fifteen miles to travel through enemy territory to reach the airfield. It's my fault you have to make that trip. Do you think I'd let you go without me?" His lips twisted. "And heaven knows, I have nothing to do but sit on my rump for the next two days. I might just as well be hiking across the country."

"Hiking," she repeated warily. "You mean we're going to be *walking*?"

"How the hell else do you think we're going to get to the airfield?"

"I do not care how we get there." She enunciated each word clearly. "Train, car, helicopter, burro. You choose. But I do *not* walk."

"This time you do," he said grimly. "I'm sorry not to have arranged to transport Your Highness more comfortably. I'm sure Bruner would have bought you a bulletproof Rolls-Royce, but I don't have his resources at present. The strip Naldona now holds between here and the airfield is very well defended, even with antiaircraft artillery. Our best and safest way is on foot through the hills. Therefore, you will walk."

"The hell I wi—" She broke off. She wouldn't be alone crossing that dangerous strip of terrain. Sandor would be with her. She didn't have the right to increase the danger to him even though it might mean discomfort or pain for her. "All right, I'll walk."

"You will?" Surprise and then amusement superseded grimness. "That was a little too easy. Why do I feel you may give me a karate chop and leave me abandoned in a ditch between here and the airfield?"

"The karate chop, maybe," she said serenely. "But I wouldn't leave you abandoned."

"That's good to know." His hand was beneath her elbow, and he nudged her gently toward his tent. "It makes me feel considerably more secure."

She paused just inside the flap of the tent, her gaze on the single cot pushed against the canvas wall. "I'm sleeping with you?" She tried to keep the tension from her voice.

"Yes." Her fingers gently touched the line of her cheek. "Sleeping. Nothing else. I want you close to me, but the other tents are too near to give us any privacy." His fingertips were feathering the corners of her mouth, and she felt a throbbing sensation wherever he touched her. "I want you to feel free to scream or moan or . . ." He bent forward to place a light kiss on the end of her nose. "Hell, I'll probably be the one who does all the groaning. You're going to drive me out of my mind." He turned away, his fingers quickly unbuttoning his shirt. "Turn out the lantern, will you?"

"All right." She moved forward a few steps and extinguished the Coleman lantern on the portable table beside the cot. "This cot isn't very wide."

"It's only a little narrower than the bed we shared last night."

"I guess so." Did she sound as breathless as she felt? She sat down on the cot and took off her shoes and socks. Her eyes were becoming accustomed to the darkness, and she could make out Sandor's shadowy figure a few feet away. "Shall I take off my clothes?"

He became very still. "I really wish you hadn't asked that. I've been trying to talk myself into total abstention and control, and I think you've just blown my arguments into shrapnel." He was coming toward her. "As much as I'd like to say yes, I think you'd better keep your clothes on, love."

"Whatever you say."

He was standing beside her, and he reached out to touch her back. "There you go again. Do you have to be so damn cooperative?"

"I feel cooperative." And excited, frightened, and more eager than ever before in her life. "I'll try to mend my ways."

"Absolutely not. Now, scoot over, Alessandra."

She moved to the far side of the cot. He settled down beside her and drew her into his arms. She inhaled sharply. He had only removed his shirt, boots, and socks, but the sudden feel of warm bare skin against her came as a shock.

"What's wrong? Did I hurt you?"

"No," she said faintly. "It was just the surprise."

"But that isn't all, is it?" His body was tense and hard against her own. "Maybe this wasn't such a good idea after all, but I didn't want to let tonight go by without grabbing something for myself." His hands were framing her face. "This damn war. There's no *time*. Do you know I haven't even kissed you yet?" Then he was rectifying the omission with sweetness and passion. The darkness was suddenly alive with warmth and magic and tenderness. He lifted his head. "Take down your hair."

"What?" she asked, wishing she could see his face. She wanted to know if his expression was as beautifully tender as his voice.

"I didn't realize your hair was so long, until I saw you in the pond. I want to touch it."

She didn't answer, but her unsteady fingers went to the pins holding her bun in place. A moment later her hair was tumbling down her back. She dropped the pins carelessly. She probably wouldn't be able to find them in the morning, but she couldn't bother to be neat now. Sandor's unsteady fingers were tangling in her loosened hair. He was pulling her closer, then closer still. His lips covered hers again, and a low moan caught in her throat. She was trembling, too. She couldn't seem to stop.

His hands were fumbling at the buttons of her blouse.

"I thought you said I wasn't supposed to get undressed," she murmured against his lips.

"I was insane. You shouldn't pay any attention to the ravings of a madman." The buttons were undone and his hands were at the front closing of her bra. "I want you in my hands. I want to feel you against me." The bra was unfastened and her breasts tumbled free from the restraint. He drew her against him. Shock and heat. Her sensitive nipples were pressed against the soft wedge of hair on his chest, and she arched up against him with a little cry.

"Shhh. It's all right."

"It's not all right." It was aching pain and need. "I can't *take* this."

"Try." His lips touched her throat with infinite gentleness. "I want you to feel you belong to me. I want you to sleep in my arms. I'm hurting, too, love."

She could tell he was speaking the truth. His muscles were tensed with a painful rigidity. "This is crazy."

His hands were gently stroking her hair. "We have to take what we can get. Tomorrow night I have to put you on a plane and get back here to receive the arms delivery." His lips brushed her forehead. "But you're right. I'm not being fair. I didn't want you to hurt too. Go to sleep, love."

She came close to laughing. How did he expect her to sleep when every muscle was tense and yearning for completion? "I'll try." She closed her eyes and firmly willed herself to sleep. It was a long time, however, before determination translated into action.

She awoke several times during the night. The first was to a delicate tugging at her nipple. She opened drowsy eyes to see Sandor's dark head over her, his lips sucking gently. "Sandor?"

He lifted his head. "Go back to sleep. Everything's fine. I can't sleep. I'm just learning you." He dropped a kiss on the nipple that had been receiving his attention. "And letting your body get to know me." His lips feathered across her half-closed lids. "It likes me."

She chuckled, her lids already closing again. She wouldn't be surprised if her body did more than like him. Each touch was so loving, it aroused an emotional as well as a physical response. She had never felt so treasured and wanted and . . .

He learned her body very well in those hours when restraint was balanced on the fine edge of desire. And she learned something about Sandor Karpathan. About his tenderness and patience and his vulnerability to her.

She awoke to find him asleep in her arms in the cool gray light preceding dawn. It seemed supremely natural to awake and find his head on her shoulder, his tanned hand clasped in possession over her naked breast. Tenderness. She felt her throat tighten helplessly as waves of emotion rocked her. She mustn't fall apart like this. How had he come to mean so much to her?

He was stirring. She grasped frantically at control. She closed her eyes. She hated pretense of any type, but she would have to pretend for the present. So far their steps toward each other had been small, almost tentative, but what she was feeling now was something different. It was such a giant leap, she refused to accept or even put a name to it. She would have to block it out. It wasn't safe to do anything else. He was coming too close.

Five

She mustn't limp. There was no reason for her to limp. She knew how to block the pain. Lord knows, she'd had plenty of experience. If she betrayed any sign of weakness, Sandor would pick up on it immediately and insist they stop. Fifteen miles, he had said. Surely they must have traveled almost that far by now. All she had to do was hold on. Soon it would be over.

"All right?" Sandor was looking over his shoulder, his gaze searching her face.

Damn. Had he noticed anything? She moistened her lips with her tongue. "Fine. Do we have much farther to go?"

"About four miles."

"That far?" She tried to smile. "I thought we'd be at the airfield by this time."

"Rough country. It makes a big difference. You've held up very well, hiking since dawn, with only a short break for lunch. You've kept up like a veteran campaigner." His eyes twinkled. "And you haven't complained once, which is truly amazing for a lady who hates to walk."

"Complaining never accomplishes anything." Her gaze narrowed on the rough trail ahead. The path wound in serpentine curves around the base of the hill before disappearing into a thick stand of pines. "The sun's going down. Do you think we'll be able to make it to the airfield before it gets dark?"

"Probably not." He turned back to the path, his stride lengthening. "But don't worry, it doesn't really matter if we don't. I know these hills."

"Do you?" Talk. He wouldn't notice anything if she talked. "They're very beautiful. It's a shame to think of battles being fought here."

"There haven't been any battles here. Naldona has always kept this strip too well fortified for us to launch an offensive against it. Even now, when his forces are at their weakest, he maintains a strong one here. We could take it now with no problem, but it has no strategic importance. It wouldn't be worth the resulting casualties."

"If it has no strategic importance, why is Naldona so determined to hold it?"

"It's my home," he said simply. He didn't look back at her, and she couldn't see his expression. Only the tension of the muscles of his shoulders revealed the emotion his tone denied. "Limtana is just a mile or so north of this hill."

"And Naldona has had control of Limtana since the beginning of the war?"

He nodded. "Bait for the trap. I was fool enough to tell him how I felt about Limtana when we were comrades-in-arms. He thinks there's a possibility

I may be an even greater fool and try to go back there." He paused. When he spoke again his voice was only a level above a whisper. "He's a very perceptive man. There have been times when I've been tempted."

"You care so much for it?"

"I love it. It's one of the things I'm fighting for. Do you know what the word nostalgia means? It's the longing for things that have been. It's a memory that causes an ache inside you. Limtana is that to me."

For a moment Alessandra felt such a surge of sympathy, she forgot the pain she was experiencing. How awful it must have been for him to love his home this much and know it was held by the enemy. "You'll be able to go back to it soon. You said yourself the war was almost over."

He was silent for a moment. Her words didn't seem to comfort him. If anything, the tension in his body intensified. "Yes, the war is almost over."

"Limtana hasn't been damaged, has it?"

"No. The castle has never been occupied and it's been kept in very good repair." His tone was sardonic. "Occasionally Naldona has even sent me a picture of it to let me see how good a caretaker he's been."

She shivered as she realized what refined torture seeing that photograph must have been for Sandor. The shiver turned to anger as heat suddenly burned through her. *Damn* Naldona. "It will be yours again." She wanted to give him back Limtana herself. The fierceness of the desire was astonishing. "Someday."

"You sound very positive." The smile he tossed over his shoulder was sad. Then the smile faded entirely as he saw the fierceness of her expression. "I can almost believe it will, which is something I haven't felt in a long, long—" He broke off, and a frown crossed his face. "You're pale. Have I been pushing you too hard?"

"No, I'm fine," she said quickly. "It's dusk. You look pale to me in this light too."

"Maybe." His gaze was keenly searching. "Still, I think we'll take a fifteen-minute break. There's a stream near here where we can wash off some of the dust."

It sounded like heaven, but if she stopped, she wasn't sure she'd be able to start again. "I think we'd better go on. We can rest when we get to the airfi—"

He wasn't listening. He was pushing his way through the shrubbery to the left of the trail, and his pace was speeding up. She had to hurry to catch up with him.

"Sandor, I really don't want to stop."

No response. He acted as if he hadn't even heard her.

"Sandor, listen to me, I—"

"Alessandra." His tone was very gentle. "Shut the hell up. You're going to rest."

It appeared she was either going to trail along with him or exhaust herself fighting the stubborn man. At the moment she was having trouble putting one foot in front of the other, and was in no shape for a major battle. Her lips tightened grimly as she followed him through the brush. But Sandor was sadly mistaken if he thought he was going to have things all his own way in their relationship. As soon as she recovered she'd have a few things to say to him about his annoying tendency to take charge.

"Here we are." Sandor unfastened his backpack and dropped it on the ground beside a thin ribbon of rushing brook. The stream looked crystal-clear, and even the low bubbling sound it made as it tumbled over the rocks was soothing. "I don't think we'd better risk drinking the water, but we can bathe our feet in it." He was pulling off his boots as he spoke. "And I, for one, am looking forward to that pleasure the way Moses did the promised land. Take your shoes and socks off and join me."

"You go ahead. I'll just wash my face and throat."

He looked up in surprise. "Don't be silly. You'll feel much better once you've soaked your feet for a while. Take off your shoes."

She shook her head. "I don't need to soak my feet. I feel great." She smiled determinedly. Why did he have to argue with her? It was difficult enough to stand here near that cool, tempting stream without having to withstand Sandor as well. She unfastened her backpack and dropped it beside Sandor's. She carefully avoided his eyes. "There. That's better."

"Alessandra."

"No!" Her tone was sharper than she had meant it to be. "I told you I didn't want to do it. Leave me alone."

"I don't think so." His hand was on her arm. "Look at me, dammit."

Her gaze lifted defiantly to his face. A flicker of apprehension went through her, which she quickly quelled. His gaze was ruthlessly analytical as it raked her features. She had a fleeting memory of the moment in her bedroom when he had told her he wouldn't have hesitated to shoot her if it had been necessary. This wasn't the Sandor who held her in his arms last night. This was the Tanzar.

"I find I'm very curious to know why you aren't willing to take off your shoes. I think I'd like to take a look at your feet." His lips tightened grimly. "It would be just like you to hide a score of blisters and not let me know."

"I don't have blisters." Her lashes lowered to veil her eyes. "Why would you think that? I haven't limped. Not once."

"Sit down. I'll take your shoes off myself."

The man was as immovable as a mountain. Well, she had to be equally determined in this case. "No. You're being ridiculous. There's no reason for you to think—"

"Alessandra, be quiet." His hands were on her shoulders, and he gave her a little shake. "Now, we can stand here and argue for the next ten minutes, and at the end of that time you'll still take off your shoes, or you can begin to fight me physically, and I'll have you down with your face in the dirt so fast it will make you dizzy." His gaze was as cool as the brook they were standing beside. "You're a strong woman, but I'm stronger. Don't make me prove it to you."

He meant exactly what he said. She couldn't hope to win a struggle with him without the advantage of surprise. She had already experienced the power in Sandor's deceptively slim body. She muttered something beneath her breath and plopped down on the bank.

"I didn't quite catch what you said, but I believe you've cast vile aspersions on my illustrious ancestors." Sandor grinned as he knelt beside her and began to unlace her left tennis shoe. His

"alluring"... "inspiring"... "irresistible"...

Loveswept

EXAMINE 4 LOVESWEPT NOVELS FOR

15 Days FREE!

Turn page for details

America's most popular, most compelling romance novels...

Loveswept

Here, at last...love stories that really involve you! Fresh, finely crafted novels with story lines so believable you'll feel you're actually living them!

Read a Loveswept novel and you'll experience all the very real feelings of two people as they discover and build an involved relationship: laughing, crying, learning and loving. Characters you can relate to... exciting places to visit...unexpected plot twists...all in all, exciting romances that satisfy your mind and delight your heart.

And now you can be sure you'll never, ever miss a single Loveswept title by enrolling in our special reader's home delivery service. A service that will bring all four new Loveswept romances published every month into your home—and deliver them to you *before* they appear in the bookstores!

Examine 4 Loveswept Novels for

15 Days FREE!

To introduce you to this fabulous service, you'll get four brand-new Loveswept releases not yet in the bookstores. These four exciting new titles are yours to examine for 15 days without obligation to buy. Keep them if you wish for just $9.95 plus postage and handling and any applicable sales tax.

SEND NO MONEY NOW.
RETURN THIS
POSTAGE-PAID CARD TODAY!

BUSINESS REPLY MAIL

FIRST-CLASS MAIL   PERMIT NO. 2456   HICKSVILLE, NY

Postage will be paid by addressee

Loveswept

Bantam Books
P.O. Box 985
Hicksville, NY 11802

former hardness had disappeared as quickly as it had come.

"I told you I don't have blisters. I don't know why you won't believe me. I didn't limp. I know I didn't limp."

"You keep repeating that." He slid the shoe off her foot and began to peel off the white sock beneath it. "I wonder why? You're very certain. It occurs to me that the only reason you could be so sure you weren't limping is because you were trying hard not to." He looked up into her mutinous face and asked quietly, "Is that what you were doing?"

"I don't have blisters."

"We'll see." He tossed the sock aside and glanced down at the foot cradled in his hand. "You have nice feet, strong and shapely."

"And large."

"Small feet would look ridiculous on a woman with your proportions." He frowned. "I don't see any blisters on your heels or toes." He started to turn her foot over to examine the sole.

"No!" She tried to jerk her foot away. "You've already seen that I don't have blisters."

It was too late. She could tell by the expression on his face: It was stunned and sick.

"No, you don't have blisters." His voice was thick. "Lord, why didn't you tell me? Is the other foot like this?"

"Yes." She tried to move her foot, but he wouldn't release it. "I'd like to put on my shoe, please."

"Not yet. You've nothing to hide anymore." He looked up to reveal eyes glittering with a terrible anger. His hands were shaking as he carefully put her left foot down and began to untie her right shoe. "You've walked over ten miles to keep your damn secret from me, but now it's out in the open." He pulled off her right shoe and sock and carefully turned her foot over and examined it. "You lied to me. This one is much worse."

She shrugged. "It doesn't hurt any more than the other one." She smiled faintly. "As far as discomfort goes they're definitely a matched set."

His hand tightened around her foot. "Don't joke. I think I could strangle you. Why didn't you *tell* me? Why didn't you put up more of an argument when I told you I was going to make you walk fifteen miles across rough country?" His eyes were blazing in his taut, pale face. "And why didn't you explain that the soles of your feet are so crisscrossed with scar tissue, it's probably impossible to walk more that *one* mile without excruciating pain?"

"You said it was safer to walk." She didn't look at him. "I didn't have a right to ask you to run any extra risks because I have a handicap."

"I would have found a way. You had no right to play the martyr." His fingers touched her scarred instep. "I feel like one of the goons in Naldona's torture squad. Dammit, why couldn't you have trusted me?" The question vibrated with impassioned force. "What the hell can I do to show you I'm worthy of your trust? You didn't have to go through this alone. I want to be there for you, but you won't let me. You hide behind your wall of silence and won't let anyone in. Well, I can't take it anymore. I'm not—" He broke off. He was shaking as if he had a chill. He closed his eyes. "Oh, dear Lord, what am I saying?" He drew a deep, shuddering breath and opened his eyes. They were still glittering, but not with anger. "I'm sorry. I didn't mean to shout at you. You've gone through enough for one day."

"You didn't shout at me." He hadn't raised his voice, but every word had been so charged with emotion, it had shocked her.

"No?" He smiled crookedly. "I felt as if I were shouting. The intent was there." He lifted her legs and swung them in a half circle, until they were dangling off the bank. "What do you say I do penance by seeing what I can do to relieve you of some of your 'discomfort'?" He moved to sit beside her on the bank. "By the way, remind me to tell you sometime how much I dislike euphemisms."

"As much as you dislike women who won't trust you?" She hadn't known she was going to ask that question. It had just tumbled out of the confusion and guilt his accusation had aroused in her.

"I thought I had made it clear I was way past being able to generalize about you." He didn't look at her as he bent over and carefully rolled up the legs of her jeans. "I can't force you to trust me. It has to come from you, and I don't dislike your lack of trust. It only . . . hurts me." He put first her left foot and then the right into the icy water of the stream. "Stay like this for a while. It will reduce the swelling and relieve the pain. Better?"

"Much better." She spoke abstractedly, her thoughts still on Sandor's words. She was barely conscious of the cool water running soothingly over her feet. She had *hurt* him. The knowledge appalled her. She hadn't meant to hurt him. She had wanted to protect him. Yet had the desire to protect been her only motive? He could be right.

The instinct to safeguard her privacy and independence had been a part of her so long, she often reacted without thinking.

But Sandor hadn't been afraid. He had the same warrior instincts she possessed, and still he had confessed his ability to be hurt by her. He had trusted her as she hadn't been able to trust him. "It happened in Said Ababa," she said abruptly.

"What?" His gaze lifted swiftly to her face.

"The scars." Her gaze was fixed on the darkening patch of sky she could see through the top of the pines. "It happened sixteen years ago in Said Ababa."

He became very still. "Sixteen years ago you would have been only twelve or thirteen years old. The wounds must have been very deep to create scar tissue like that." He tried to keep his tone expressionless, desperately afraid she would close up again.

"They were deep. They became infected. I was lucky I didn't get gangrene. Antibiotics were practically nonexistent at the camp." She moistened her lower lip with her tongue. "I probably would have died if it hadn't been for Dimitri."

"Camp?"

"I was in a displaced-persons' camp for two years in Said Ababa." The words were halting, and corroded with the years of repression. "After the overthrow of the government, the revolutionaries took power. They were even more oppressive than the tyrants they'd replaced."

"So I've heard." Horror stories had emerged by the hundreds after the revolution, Sandor remembered. And Alessandra had been in the center of that relentless reign of terror. "You're an American. How did you come to be in a displaced-persons' camp?"

"I didn't say I was an American. I said I hold an American passport. I didn't have any passport or any identification at all after the revolution. I could have been any nationality. James said there was a good possibility I was an American, because one of the government officials who ran the camp said he thought he remembered seeing me wandering in the streets of the company town near the American oil refinery." She shrugged. "There was some doubt. The town was several hundred miles from where they picked me up. I was barefoot and out of my head with fever, lying by the side of the road. James says walking that distance through the mountains and desert could have been the cause of my lacerated feet."

"James 'says,'" he repeated slowly. "Don't you know?"

"No. I don't remember anything before I woke up in the camp. That was why it was difficult to pinpoint my nationality. I spoke English, French, and German fluently. The oil refinery and the town itself were destroyed by the bombing." Her voice lowered. "They tell me the town burned for four days and you could see the flames clawing at the sky from a distance of over a hundred miles."

Clawing at the sky. The phrase evoked a vivid picture of desperation and terror. Had someone really used those words or had a wisp of memory managed to filter through the barriers a young woman had erected to protect herself from an experience too terrible to remember?

"There was a protest from the American government at the time," Sandor said. "But they had airlifted most of the personnel who were American citizens out of the area before the situation came to a boil. Weren't there any inquiries about you?"

She shook her head. "There were no records and no inquiries. It's not unusual, when you think about it. There are thousands of people in the world who have cut themselves off from their roots. Maybe my parents were a part of that group."

"I didn't realize there was a displaced-persons' camp in Said Ababa," Sandor prompted gently. He wanted to fire questions and rip aside the barriers. Patience. It was a miracle she had told him as much as she had. It was obviously very difficult for her.

"There wasn't a camp for over a year after the revolution. The government was getting flak from several humanitarian groups, and the camp was established to quiet the criticism." Her lips twisted. "Dimitri said the concentration camp he was sent to in Poland as a boy was more humane."

It was the second time she had mentioned the name. "Dimitri?"

"Dimitri Sokol, my friend. When I woke up, his was the first face I saw. He took care of me until I was able to walk again. He gave me half his rations because I wasn't able to keep the other prisoners from stealing the food the guards issued me. He protected me as much as he could." She slowly shook her head. "Which wasn't very much. Dimitri didn't understand the world he'd been born into. He was the gentlest human being I've ever known. He was a scholar, and had been a professor at a university in Warsaw. You would have thought the study of history would have taught him that you have to fight to survive. Saints are usually the first to be martyred."

"And was your Dimitri a saint?"

"No, only a man. A kind and generous . . ." Her voice broke. "I don't want to talk about Dimitri."

"Then don't talk about him." His hand reached out to cover her own on the grass. "Don't talk about anything, if you don't want to."

She was silent for a few minutes. Dimitri was part of it. She couldn't leave Dimitri out of the story and still give . . . She forced herself to speak. "When I was well again, he didn't have to worry about protecting me. I was the one who took care of him. I was young and strong and I knew how to survive." Her voice was fierce. "No one dared steal his rations or mine after I showed what would happen to them if they tried. They were animals. The war had made them animals. Do you know the key to surviving in a world of animals?"

"No." He didn't know if she even heard him. He had an idea she wasn't there with him anymore.

"You have to let them know you mean every word you say. If you commit yourself, it has to be with the knowledge that it will be followed up by action. I learned all the moves and developed a few of my own. Most of the time Dimitri didn't realize what was going on. I don't think he wanted to live in a jungle world. I even had to stop him from giving away the food I'd fought to keep. I made sure he had blankets, that he ate, that he exercised. He told me stories and taught me lessons, and even made me laugh. He kept me human. I would have turned into an animal like the rest of them if it hadn't been for Dimitri. Do you know he even gave me my name? The camp officials hadn't bothered. I was just inmate 534. Dimitri said beautiful words lift the heart and I must have a beautiful name so every time I heard it I would know joy. We spent two days choosing it. It was during one of the bad times, and I think he only persisted to try to take my mind off what was going on around me." Her voice was just above a whisper. "He gave me so much more than I gave him, and he didn't even realize it."

Sandor felt his throat tighten. "You probably gave him more than you knew. You loved him. He must have known that."

"Yes, he knew I loved him. We never talked about love. It seemed foreign in that place. But he knew." She closed her eyes. "Oh, Lord, I hope he knew. I didn't think he needed the words, but maybe he did. Maybe he died and didn't know how much—"

"No." Sandor's voice was firm and totally reassuring. "You're right. Sometimes words aren't necessary. Dimitri knew how you felt." Dimitri had died. Sandor had to find a way to shift the subject away from him. He could feel the pain radiating from her. "When did you meet Bruner?"

"The day Dimitri died."

What a stupid blunder to have made. He tried to think of a way to ease her away from the memories, but it was too late. She was back in that hideous hellhole, and her voice held all the pain of a lost soul. "There weren't any antibiotics, did I tell you that? I did everything I could think of to keep him well, but he caught a chill and developed pneumonia. I tried to make the guards get him the medicine he needed. I *screamed* at them. He was dying, and they wouldn't listen to me." Her nails were biting into his hand. "All I could do was stay with him and watch him struggle to get his breath. He lasted for five days."

"Alessandra . . ."

"I think I went crazy. I wanted to kill someone. He was the only good thing in my life and they had let him die. I screamed like a lunatic. I attacked a guard. We were cursing and rolling around in the dirt of the yard, and I remember how surprised the guard looked. They had let Dimitri die and I was just supposed to accept it." Her voice held a note of wonder. "You would have thought they'd know I couldn't do that."

"No." He ached to take her in his arms and hold her. "You wouldn't be able to do that."

"James was touring the camp that day, and he saw me struggling with the guard. He stopped the other guards from hurting me when they managed to pull me away from him." She opened her eyes. "He talked to me for a long time. I don't remember what he said. He did arrange to have a proper burial for Dimitri. He told me later I'd asked him to do that. I didn't remember. All I knew was that Dimitri was dead and I was alone again. James came back the next day and we talked. He kept coming back day after day. Then he told me he had made arrangements for me to leave the camp and come to live with him at his hotel until he could get me papers to leave Said Ababa."

Sandor felt a quick flare of anger. "They just turned you over to him?" He tried to keep from his tone the raw, possessive rage the thought evoked. He had no right to feel this damnable jealousy. Choices. He knew how ugly some of the choices had to be. Better Bruner's mistress than that monstrosity of a camp.

She nodded. "The government wanted a favor. His company had sold them arms to fight their revolution. Now they were looking across the border at Sedikhan and wanted him to sell them enough arms to launch an invasion force. He wasn't about to do it, but he stalled them until he could get me out of the country." She fell silent, and the only sound in the shadow-shrouded forest was the rushing of the brook and the soft whirring of the cicadas. "Is it enough?"

He frowned in puzzlement. "Is what enough?"

For the first time since she had begun to speak, her gaze left the patch of sky above the pines to meet his own. "I've never told anyone about Said Ababa. It was the only way I could think of to show you I do trust you. Do you need me to tell you any more?"

He felt as if he were slowly disintegrating inside. She had relived that hell to give him a *gift*? He couldn't look at her. "I don't need to know any more," he said gruffly. "Lord, yes, it's enough." He released her hand and bent down to lift her feet out of the water. "Your feet must be ice blocks by now."

"They don't hurt anymore." She watched as Sandor took his handkerchief from his back pocket and began to dry her feet. It was an intimate gesture that filled her with poignant tenderness. "I won't have any trouble making it to the airfield now."

"No?" His tone was abstracted. He cradled one foot in his hands. "Poor mermaid."

"Mermaid?"

"There's a fairy tale about a sorceress who cast a spell to permit a mermaid to assume a human form and come live among mortals. Unfortunately, it was very painful for the mermaid to stay ashore. When she walked, it was as if she were stepping on knives."

"Well, I'm no mermaid, and I can walk very well. It's almost dark. Don't you think we should be on our way?"

"Yes." He was still looking down at her foot. He caressed her ankle. "Put on your shoes and socks." He began to pull on his own boots.

"I thought you wanted to bathe your feet," she said as she began to put on her socks.

"It doesn't matter." He stood up and began to fasten his backpack. "I can wait. It's not that far."

"Four miles through the hills? Far enough." She finished tying the laces of her shoes. "A few minutes more won't make any difference. Why don't you—"

"Come on." He pulled her to her feet, reached down and picked up her knapsack, and handed it to her. "We're not going to be walking another four miles tonight." He didn't look at her as he began to lead her through the underbrush. "We're going to Limtana."

Six

"It looks like Sleeping Beauty's castle," Alessandra whispered. She stood abreast of Sandor on the summit of a hill and looked down into the valley below. The gray stone castle, with its crenellated towers, appeared both grand and desolate. The grounds surrounding it had been let go, vines and shrubs forming a labyrinth. "It's as if the castle has been sleeping for a hundred years."

"Only a little over two." Sandor's lips twisted. "Naldona's caretaking evidently didn't include the grounds." He turned away. "Come on."

"No!" Her hands clenched into fists at her sides. "You said yourself the castle was bait for a trap. It looks deserted, but that doesn't necessarily mean it is. Naldona could have men stationed on lookout to report back to him if they see someone."

"I'm sure he does, but they won't see anyone." He glanced back over his shoulder. "You're a very argumentative woman. Do we have to go over it all again? I'm not about to make you walk another four miles, after the pace I set today. We'll start out at dawn, once you've had a chance to rest."

"But it's *stupid.* Can't you see that? If you insist we stop for the night, let's camp here in the hills. It's not safe for you down there in that castle."

"For me?" His face softened. "Do you know that's the first time you've said anything to indicate you might be the tiniest bit upset if Naldona managed to cut my throat, as he's been promising?"

"Of course I'd be upset." She scowled at him. "Though you'd deserve it for being so foolish."

He chuckled. "No one could accuse you of being overly sentimental. Men in my particular state are often foolish. All the poets say so." His smile faded. "I want you to see my home, Alessandra. It's important to me. I can't promise it will be absolutely safe, but I wouldn't run the risk if I didn't have an edge."

He was asking her to trust him again. He didn't say the words, but the implication was there. And she knew she was going to do it, she thought with resignation. "Oh, all right." She gestured for him to lead the way. "But your edge had better be damned sharp, Sandor."

He was leading her toward a clump of rocks a few yards away. "It's one you've experienced before, though I don't believe you recall it with any degree of pleasure." He bent down, his fingers exploring the weed-covered ground. "Ah, here it is." He pulled upward. Earth and weeds rose to reveal a neat hole approximately three feet square.

"A trapdoor." Alessandra slowly shook her head in resignation. "Don't tell me. A secret passageway. Right?"

"Right."

"I wonder why you Tamrovians even bother to build streets. You seem to be so fond of crawling around underground."

"Don't be sarcastic, love. Every respectable castle has to have a secret passage. It's part of our local color." He gestured. "After you. Hold fast to the railing in case the stairs are slippery. You see how civilized we are here in Limtana? No crude ladder, like the sewer in Belajo. Real stairs."

"I'm impressed," she said as she took a tentative step into the darkness. "However, I'll be more impressed if you tell me your 'color' is completely rodent-free."

"Well . . ." His lips lightly feathered her ear as he followed her down the steps. "As much as I'd like to reassure you, the last time I was down here was when I was ten years old. I can't vouch for the rats." He closed the trapdoor and flicked on the flashlight. His blue eyes were dancing in the soft glow illuminating the darkness. "But I can promise you Limtana is guaranteed to be alligator-free."

His expression reminded her of the mischievous ten-year-old he must have been when he used this passage as a playground. The cynical lines and weariness she had thought permanently carved in his face were entirely gone. "You're happy," she said softly. "Why are you so happy?"

"I'm home." He gently nudged her forward. "I had a wonderful time in these passages when I was a boy. They were a family secret, so I couldn't bring any of the servants' children down here to play with me. It didn't really matter, though. Down here I could pretend I was anything I wanted to be. I had a huge Irish setter named Boris, and he would skid along this passage like a . . ."

The words and remembrances flowed over her on the mile-long walk down the stairs and through the long tunnel. Confidences, experiences, childhood practical jokes. He seemed to want to share them all with her. She found herself listening with amusement and an odd, maternal tenderness. And then they were climbing a long flight of steps again and she glanced over her shoulder. "Where does the passage exit?"

"In the nursery. I found it quite convenient."

"I imagine you did." She smiled gently. "You must have had a very happy childhood."

He nodded. "I was lucky. I had two parents who loved each other and loved me, a home that was all a home should be, the whole countryside to run wild in. I was damned lucky to—" he broke off, his expression clouding. "Lord, I'm sorry. I didn't think. You must think I'm an insensitive bastard."

"Because I didn't have all those things?" She shook her head. "Perhaps I did. I don't know what my life was like before the revolution in Said Ababa. Perhaps life was very good for me too. I hope it was."

"But you don't remember." His expression was somber. "Haven't there been times when you wanted those memories back?"

"No." Her voice was low, but firm. "What I'd gain wouldn't be worth what I might lose. I've had enough nightmares in my life without risking more. I am what I am. A background and a family tree couldn't change me now."

And sometimes there were reasons for the mind to erect barriers, he thought. She was probably right not to try to resurrect the past. There was too much danger of those memories being tragic. "A family tree can be something of a bore anyway." He carefully kept his tone light as he drew even with her at the top of the stairs. "I'm weighed down by the branches of my noble ancestors. I'll be glad to share them with you." He met her gaze with sudden gravity. "I'll be glad to share everything with you. My childhood, my memories, the love I knew and still know. There's nothing frightening in my past." His voice was velvet-soft. "Let me share those good times with you, Alessandra."

Her throat was so tight, she found it difficult to swallow. She blinked back tears. Tanzar. The one who is all. Gentleness, strength, laughter, sensitivity.

"That's . . . very kind of you." The words were awkward and pitifully inadequate but all she was capable of at the moment. "I don't know what to say." She smiled shakily. "I don't think there are any books written about how to accept a gift of that magnitude."

"You just accept it." He kissed her cheek with infinite tenderness. "As I give it. With all my love."

Love. She stiffened with shock. This wasn't the casual endearment he had used before. Her gaze flew to meet his with a sudden sense of panic. "Sandor, I don't know—"

"Shh." His fingers covered her lips. "Not now. I know it's too soon. Just think about it. Okay?"

How could she help thinking about it? She nodded jerkily. "Okay."

"Good." He reached around her to the knob on the blank wall facing them. It took a little tugging, but the panel finally slid far enough for them to sidle through the opening. "Well, at least we know Naldona hasn't discovered the passage. For a moment I thought we'd have to chop our way through the wall." It took him as long to tug the panel back in place as it had to open it.

"Can I help?"

"No, I think I've got it." He slid the panel the last few inches and turned to face her with a slightly droll smile. "Maybe I should have used the passage more frequently after I reached adolescence. I don't remember it being this difficult to budge when I was a child." The ray of the flashlight danced around the dusty room. "And I remember this nursery as being larger."

"Have you ever considered that you might have been smaller?" Alessandra asked solemnly, her lips twitching.

"Possibly." The beam suddenly pinpointed something across the room. "But some things stay the same. Come on, I want to introduce you to Leo."

"Leo?"

"My rocking horse." He was striding quickly across the room. "It belonged to my great-great-grandfather and was passed down from father to son. It was always my favorite toy."

The large wooden rocking horse was a dappled gray with a black mane, sporting an embossed red saddle and gay golden tassels hanging from the bridle. His dark painted eyes appeared to glow, and there was an eager smile painted on his lips. "He's wonderful," Alessandra said softly. "He looks as if he's ready to waltz off to another adventure just over the horizon. Why is he called Leo? Isn't that name usually reserved for lions?"

Sandor nodded. His hand ran caressingly over the black mane. "My father said he has the heart of a lion. He gave Leo to me when I was four years old. He told me his history and the history of all the Karpathans who had ridden him over the years." He pointed to a deep scratch beside the right stirrup. "My grandfather did that. One morning he crept into his father's room and stole the spurs off his boots. He didn't see why he couldn't have spurs to ride his horse too." Sandor tugged at one tassel. "In some ways he was more real to me than the live pony my father gave me a year later."

"From father to son. What a lovely tradition." She moved a step closer and touched the saddle with a tentative finger. It was foolish, but she felt almost as if the wooden horse were alive. He had witnessed so much love, heard so much laughter, experienced so many imaginary adventures with his small friends. Now he was in this abandoned nursery, resting but not forgotten. Waiting for the next child to come. "Someday you'll give him to your son." There was a silence. When she looked up, it was to see that Sandor was no longer smiling. "Is something wrong?"

"No." He gave the tassel another tug. "Nothing's wrong. Let me show you the rest of my home. How are your feet?"

"A little sore. Nothing serious."

"I won't keep you on them very long." His gaze traveled around the room, and his expression revealed his feelings of melancholy mixed with affection. "There are a few things I want you to see"—he paused—"and that I want to see again with you. Then I'll let you bathe and go to bed."

"I want to see everything," she said quickly. "You promised to share with me, and I'm holding you to it." If she'd been ready to drop from exhaustion, her response would have been the same. She had an instinctive feeling Sandor needed to share his past even more than she needed to accept the gift. "I don't suppose we dare turn on any lights."

"No, I imagine the main generator is turned off, but there are plenty of candles lying about. My mother loved candlelight. If we're careful to draw the drapes before we light the candles, there shouldn't be any danger." He opened the door and bowed with half-mocking grandeur. "Step into my world, milady."

And for the next hour she felt as if, in some mysterious fashion, she had done just that. The conversation was light and the laughter frequent as they wandered down the polished halls and through the rooms that all appeared to have a story or hold a special memory for Sandor. She found her gaze clinging to his face in a sort of wonder. Lord, he'd loved this place. Affection was lighting his face with an incandescent glow far brighter than the flickering candlelight.

"My mother liked this vase. My father gave—" He broke off. "Why are you looking at me like that?" He grinned sheepishly. "I guess I've been pretty talkative, haven't I?"

She shook her head. "I've enjoyed it. I've enjoyed *you*, Sandor."

He looked surprised, and then a flush darkened his cheeks. Good heavens, he was embarrassed. Even his shrug was a little awkward. "That was my intention. But, as your American colloquialism goes, 'You ain't seen nothing yet.' "

"I haven't?" Her eyes twinkled. "I've seen the scullery, the dungeon, the study, the grand ballroom, the front parlor, the garden room, the—"

"You haven't seen the master bedroom yet."

Her breath stopped in her throat, and she had to part her lips to get more air into her lungs. "No, I haven't."

"I saved it for the last." His eyes gravely met her own. "Because we won't be leaving there again tonight, will we?"

"No." The dimness of the hall was lit only by the candelabrum Sandor was carrying. The pool of light it cast around them reminded her of an intimate spotlight. Intimate. Her heart was suddenly pounding wildly, and her breasts were lifting and falling with every breath she drew. "I guess we won't."

She could see the tenseness leave him, the rigidity flowing out. Had he thought she was going to refuse him? It seemed incredible. They had been building toward this final intimacy since the moment they met. The knowledge was filling her with an exuberance she had never known before. He was looking at her with the same eagerness as he had Leo a short time before. She smothered a sudden gurgle of laughter.

"Why are you laughing?" His expression revealed that he was experiencing the same giddy exhilaration she was. "Should my manly pride be hurt? I don't believe I've ever encountered that reaction when I asked a woman to go to bed with me."

"I was just thinking how happy I was that you like me as much as you do Leo," she said teasingly. "And I was wondering if someday I might dare to aspire even higher."

His fingers lightly touched the tip of her nose. "You've already passed Leo at the post. I never invited him into the master bedroom."

"Thank heavens for that."

"Brat." This time the tap on her nose was admonishing. "For that matter, I've never invited anyone into the master bedroom. After my father died and my mother returned to Argentina, I didn't bother to move from my old room. The master suite didn't seem to belong to me." His smile faded. "But tonight I want very much to sleep in the bed where my father and his father slept. And I want you to sleep there with me. Is that all right with you?"

It was too difficult to speak; every nerve and muscle in her body was shaking like a willow frond in a windstorm. She nodded, then tore her gaze away from Sandor and veiled her eyes with her lashes. Shy. Good Lord, she felt shy.

His hand on her elbow came as a little shock. The touch wasn't lightly teasing, as before. It was a caress as possessive as a kiss. "I promised you a bath." He was gently propelling her toward the carved double doors at the end of the hall. "I'm afraid it will have to be a cold one—the hot-water heater would have to be lit, and that would take longer. . . ."

"I don't mind." Why was he talking about hot-water heaters? she wondered wildly. "It's not as if it were winter."

"No." He opened the door to let her precede him. "Personally, I've had enough cold water to last me for quite a while." A tiny twinkle appeared in his eyes. "The water yesterday in the pond may have cooled my libido, but I'm glad I won't have to indulge in any further spartan aquatics for that particular reason." He glanced around the bedroom. "I'm afraid this room is as dusty as the rest of the castle. I'll change the sheets on the bed and see if I can tidy up a little after I take my shower." He nodded to the door across the room. "There's the dressing room and master bathroom. I'll go to one of the guest rooms and shower." He held out the silver candelabrum. "You'd better take this. I won't have any problem finding my way around in the dark."

No, he wouldn't have any trouble, she thought tenderly. Every inch of this place was graven in his heart and memory. She took the candelabrum. "Thank you. I'll try not to be long."

"I'll wait. I'm not going anywhere." His eyes were warm and glowingly intent. "You'd have to point a nuclear missile at me to drive me away."

"I don't have any missiles tucked away anywhere, so I guess it's safe." She turned away, avoiding his eyes. She didn't feel safe. She was tottering on the edge of something new and unknown, and she had never felt more frightened in her life. "I'll be right back."

"Alessandra."

She glanced back over her shoulder to see him frowning at her.

"What's wrong? Don't you want me?"

Tenderness rushed over her. With one word she could hurt him terribly. It was there in the open vulnerability of his expression. She was closing him out again because she was afraid. Perhaps if she could force herself to share her fear as he had shared his past . . . She turned to face him. "I want you." She gazed directly at him. "There's something you should know. I'm not experienced. I may not be able to please you." She lifted her chin. "At first. But if you'll help me, I promise I'll

make up for it later. I learn fast, and I'll be compe-
tent in no time." She was speaking rapidly, the
words tumbling over one another. Slowly. She
wasn't a child, to be this nervous. "I know you
must have had all kinds of affairs, and you may
not want to—" She broke off. "Why don't you say
something?"

"I'm trying to take it in," he said blankly.
"Bruner?"

"You said once that I was probably going to be
your hair shirt. You were joking, but that's what I
am to James." She shook her head sadly. "He's a
good man. He inherited the factory from his father and never really knew what war was all about
until he visited Said Ababa after the revolution. It
really came home to him then—the wars and the
misery he had helped to create by indiscriminate
munitions sales he had made. I think, in some
ways, I became a symbol for him. His penance. If he
could make everything right for me, then maybe
he could assuage the guilt he felt about all the
rest. When I brought up my idea about helping
the children, he jumped at it."

"But why no one else? You're a very responsive
woman."

She shrugged. "I don't know why. Maybe you're
right. It could be that I didn't trust anyone enough
to let him get that close to me." She paused.
"Until now."

He experienced a joy so intense, he could scarcely
contain it. Joy and a sudden apprehension just
as intense. What if he fouled up and disappointed
her? "You really believe in loading responsibility
on a man, don't you, love?"

"Oh, no." Her eyes widened in surprise. "I didn't

want you to feel responsible. I just thought you should know." She rushed on. "I'm not even a virgin. When James took me out of the camp, he was given the record of the examination the doctor gave me when they brought me there." She frowned like an earnest little girl. "I'm quite normal, but I wasn't a virgin."

She was trying to reassure *him*. She'd been only twelve years old when she had entered the camp. Oh, Lord, don't let her ever remember that time before. He felt a hot stinging behind his lids and had to transfer his gaze from her face to the flickering flame of a candle. "I'll make a deal with you," he said gruffly. "Suppose you be responsible for me and I'll be responsible for you. I don't mind responsibility. I'm beginning to like the idea." He turned away. "I hope you'll learn to like it too."

She gazed at the door in bemusement after it closed behind him. Responsibility. It was such a heavy word. Yet it had sounded warm and beautiful, the way Sandor had said it, and there was nothing heavy about the way it made her feel. Her step was as light as the zinging exhilaration floating through her veins as she turned and moved quickly toward the door of the dressing room.

Seven

The exquisite square of patterned silk was folded neatly beside the candelabrum she had set on the marble-topped vanity. It was the first thing Alessandra saw when she stepped out of the shower stall and reached for the towel on the rack beside it. There was a brief note lying on the top of the silk.

> It belongs to my mother. She would want you to wear it.
>
> S.

It was the second note she had received from Sandor. Who could have imagined when she had been given that first tension-charged directive that within forty-eight hours she would be reading this entirely different and intimate message? She hurriedly finished drying and tossed the towel aside.

She could hardly wait to shake out that alluring heap of colorful silk.

It was a shawl. Not a token bit of material, but a full shawl such as she had seen worn by Spanish flamenco dancers. The white silk background had been mellowed to a rich ivory by years of loving use. The once-brilliant blossoms of the print had faded to a delicate shade of pink, and the thick, eight-inch silk fringe bordering it gleamed and flowed in the candlelight. Beautiful. The shawl was like Sandor's home, old and lovely and cared for with great love and devotion. In a world filled with disposable items and disposable relationships, it was rare and wonderful to find a family whose devotion to one another and their possessions only increased as time passed.

She hurriedly brushed her hair until it shone and rippled in rich brown waves over her shoulders. Then she draped the shawl about her, leaving her shoulders bare. The silk triangle was so large, the fringe brushed against her mid-thighs and the folds completely enveloped her in its rich beauty.

She *felt* beautiful. Her fingers lovingly touched the silk fringe. Being physically attractive had never been high on her list of priorities, but she was suddenly passionately grateful for this illusion of beauty she'd been given. She wanted to be beautiful for Sandor tonight.

She clutched the shawl together over her breasts with one hand and opened the door with the other. "Sandor?"

"Right here."

She had known he would be there waiting for

her. Sandor would always be there to help and succor when she needed him. Always? The word had come naturally to mind, but she mustn't think of always. Sometimes a moment could be enough. She turned to pick up the candelabrum from the vanity and entered the bedroom.

He was already in bed, leaning against the carved headboard of the enormous bed with a sheet draped carelessly over his naked hips. Naked. She stopped abruptly in the middle of the room. She drew a deep breath and tried to stop the trembling of her hand clasping the silver candelabrum. Of course he was naked. What else had she expected? "Thank you for letting me use your mother's shawl. It's absolutely magnificent. I'm surprised she didn't take it with her."

"It's one of her favorite shawls. Our family believes that when you depart from a place or a person you love, you should always leave a treasured object behind to retain possession. It's a common tradition here in Tamrovia. It's called the *casimar*, the homing."

"The homing," she echoed softly. "What is your mother's given name?"

"Mariana. Why?"

"No reason." Thank you, Mariana. For the use of the shawl, the *casimar*, and, most of all, for this man sitting looking at her with a warm intentness more gentle than the candlelight. "I just wondered." She set the candelabrum on the table beside her. "Shall I blow out the candles?"

"No. I want to see you." He suddenly chuckled. "I've spent two nights in the dark in bed with you. I think it's time for a change, don't you?"

"If you do." She moistened her lower lip with her tongue as she climbed the three steps to stand beside the bed. "I didn't mind lying in bed in the dark with you. It was very . . . nice."

"Nice." A little smile tugged at his lips. "What a stilted understatement. Are you, by any chance, a little nervous, love?"

"A little," she admitted, not looking at him. "I don't know what you expect of me."

He tugged at the fringe of the shawl. "Look at me." His expression was grave. "I expect to enjoy you and I expect you to enjoy me. That's what this is all about." He paused before adding softly, "Joy."

She felt a melting deep within her. "I think I can handle that."

"You can handle anything." His eyes were twinkling. "And I give you full permission to do it. My humble person is at your service." His hand covered her hand clutching the shawl over her breasts and gently unclenched it. "I'll take care of this. I want you to have your hands free." He threw aside the sheet and swiveled to a sitting position on the side of the bed so she was standing between his legs.

She inhaled sharply. She suddenly felt very vulnerable standing here in near-nakedness, held captive by his hand on the silk at her breast. Vulnerable and tingling and . . . The soft hair dusting his thighs was pressing against her smooth skin, and his eyes were darkening with the same tension that was causing her breasts to lift and fall with every breath.

His hand moved slowly to the fringe brushing

her thighs. "Do you know how lovely you are?" His voice was hoarse. "You look as sensual as the Delacroix painting of his Odalisque. When you walked through that door, I wanted you so much, I thought it would kill me."

"'You appeared very . . ." His hand was moving the veil of fringe aside, and the touch of his warm fingertips on her inner thigh caused her to flinch with surprise. "Calm."

"Did I? I don't even remember what I said. All I could think of were those lovely legs and what was waiting between them." He had found what was waiting between them. "So soft," he murmured, his fingers moving in gentle exploration. "I think your fringe is more silky than the shawl's."

"Sandor." She could barely force the word out through the tightness of her throat. What his fingers were doing to her was causing jolts of electricity through every muscle of her body. "I can't . . ."

"Shh, I know." His hand clutching the silk over her breasts loosened barely enough to let the shawl slip from her shoulders to just below her breasts. He tightened his grip and the band of silk lifted her breasts into bold prominence. His gaze was hot and intent as it fastened on the full, swollen mounds jutting from their bed of silk. "Let me suckle, love." His head was moving slowly toward her. "Pleasure me. As I will pleasure you." His fingers plunged deep as his open mouth closed over her nipple.

Alessandra's head jerked back. She gave a low moan, her hands clutching wildly at his shoulders for support. Her legs felt as if they would collapse at any second. The steady hungry suckling at her breast was incredibly erotic, and the rhythm of his fingers . . .

"Are you ready for me?" His teeth gently pulled at her nipple. "Lord, love, say you're ready for me." He began suckling at her other breast, his tongue moving over her. He lifted his head. "I hate to leave these pretty things, but if I don't get inside you I'm going to go insane. Are you rea—"

"Yes," she interrupted. "Yes!"

"Then, come." He pulled her down astride him. With one jerk, the shawl was no longer around her, but tossed on the chair beside the bed. His lips covered her own with an urgency that held an element of pain. His tongue entered her mouth as he shifted her body to attain another entrance.

Her nails dug into the flesh of his shoulders as she felt the teasing abrasion of his hair-roughened chest against her sensitive nipples. His breathing was harsh, as if he were running, and she heard him give a low groan of hunger against her lips.

With one plunge they were together. Fullness. Heat. *Casimar.* She was the one who was groaning now. The sensation was incredible. She wanted more. Her hips moved yearningly, and then she had to stop as a shudder of pleasure shook her. He felt so *right* within her.

His palm was slowly rubbing the tight curls surrounding him. "Such a lovely fringe." His voice was so thick, it was nearly gutteral. "Such a lovely Alessandra. I'd like to wear *you* as a shawl." He was falling sidewise on the bed and his hips were moving with frantic urgency. "I want you around me." She gasped as he plunged deeper. "In me.

Over me. I want you to become so much a part of me that—" He broke off. His face was heavy with sensuality and a pained pleasure as he moved with increasing force and passion.

Every breath she drew was a gasp and every touch was a shock as the tension grew. She felt as if he were tearing her apart, cleaving her with the violence of their passion. Yet his actions held no violence but that of sheer intensity. He rolled over on his back, and his hands on her hips moved her, shifting her over him. His lips opened to catch at her nipple as he lifted his hips to plunge upward.

She couldn't breathe. She was too full. Too full of joy. Too full of hunger. Too full of Sandor.

He was moving faster, deeper, and the tension was growing. She couldn't take any more. Yet she did, and still found herself reaching out again and again. Then there was no more to accept, only the radiant explosion of sensation and the treasure left behind to retain an eternal possession. *Casimar.*

Sandor's eyes were closed, and his chest was heaving with the harshness of his breathing. His hands were still holding her hips, and she could see the pulse continuing to pound wildly in the hollow of his throat. "Lord, you're wonderful."

"*We're* wonderful." She was suddenly giddy with happiness. She wanted to laugh or shout. "I think it was fair to say this was a joint operation." She glanced down, her lips twitching. "Particularly since our togetherness still very obviously exists."

He opened his eyes. "Not as obviously as a moment ago, unfortunately." His hands encircled her breasts. "But I think in this case we can expect an astounding restoration in no time at all. Come here."

His tongue flicked lazily at one pink nipple as she bent forward. She felt a flexing and then a deep stirring within her that corresponded with the rebirth of the tension she had thought was gone from her own body. The pleasure was going to begin again. She experienced a flicker of excitement like the first spark that will eventually ignite a blaze. Yet there was something she wanted to say to him, feelings she wanted to put into words, about the joy he had given her.

"Sandor, I want to tell you—"

"Later, love." He was rolling over her on the bed and looking down at her with eyes that held glowing tenderness as well as hunger. "We can talk later. This is more important now."

"Yes." She closed her eyes and let emotion sweep her away. He was right. This was what was important. Words could come later. "Oh, yes."

She was sleeping. Sandor carefully shifted her to one side and took his arms from around her. Alessandra muttered a half-audible protest, and he froze into stillness. A moment later her breathing resumed its even tenor. He drew the sheet up about her shoulders and brushed a light kiss on her forehead. Then he slipped from the bed and dressed quickly. He moved silently across the room toward the bedroom door.

Damn! He didn't want to leave Alessandra. He was tempted to turn around and slip back into bed and take her in his arms again. Their time together had been so damnably brief. Surely it wouldn't hurt to . . . No, he couldn't go back to her. He had been foolishly reckless to take this chance and bring her to Limtana. He had known at the time, but he had wanted this time with her in his home. The memory might have to last him for the rest of his life. He had to accept the risk he had run and couldn't indulge himself any further tonight. There hadn't been any sign of Naldona's men, but he had to be sure. He would take a final look around the grounds to make certain before he allowed himself to return to her. Alessandra must be safeguarded.

He opened the door and cast another quick glance over his shoulder. He felt a sudden poignant pang of tenderness. She looked as vulnerable as a sleeping child in the huge bed. He stood there a moment, just looking at her. Then he softly closed the door behind him.

"Wake up, Alessandra. We have to get the hell out of here."

The web of sleep was torn with an abruptness that brought Alessandra bolt upright in bed. "What is it?"

Sandor strode out of the bathroom and tossed her clothes on the bed. He had turned on the flashlight, and his face was taut and hard in its faint glow. "Get dressed. There's something happening out there, and I don't like it."

"What?" She jumped out of bed and began dressing swiftly. "A guard?"

He nodded. "Very much in the plural, judging by the voices I heard in the garden." His lips tightened. "I didn't stay to count them after I saw a helicopter start to land."

"Reinforcements? But how could they know we're here?"

"I have no idea. We'll worry about that after we're gone. Ready?"

She nodded as she snatched up her knapsack. "Let's go."

He was already at the door. He stopped her by placing his hand on her arm. "This isn't what I planned," he said quietly. "I wanted this night to be as perfect for you as it was for me."

Good Lord, was he *apologizing* at a moment like this? Then her impatience was submerged in tenderness. She had a lot to learn. When danger surfaced, she had instinctively pushed the experience they had shared to the rear of her consciousness, as if it hadn't existed. Sandor had obviously been even more conscious of the danger than she, and yet he hadn't allowed it to diminish what they'd had together. "There are a few advantages to being awakened in the middle of the night," she said with a smile. "I won't have to wonder when I wake up in the morning if you still respect me."

"I'll respect you. Tonight, tomorrow, for the rest of our lives." His kiss was quick and hard. "Now let's get out of here, or the rest of our lives may be very brief."

They were halfway down the hall when they heard the voice; loud, hollow, and slightly distorted by the megaphone. "Karpathan!"

Sandor muttered a curse.

"It sounded so close," Alessandra whispered. "Are they in the castle?"

"'Downstairs in the entrance hall, by the sound of it. Or at least *he* is."

The voice came again, slightly mocking. "Come and talk to me, Karpathan. You're in no danger at the moment. I have something special and entirely fitting planned for you."

She knew that voice. "It's Naldona," Alessandra said, shocked.

Sandor nodded. "The helicopter. He obviously couldn't resist the temptation to come and close the trap himself." He turned and began striding down the hall toward the main staircase. "Stay here."

"You're going down there? They'll kill you!"

"We need time. I don't want them rushing us." He cast her a reassuring smile. "I'm not going downstairs. I'll stand at the top of the stairs and talk to him." He flicked out the flashlight. "And I'll make damn sure the hall is in complete darkness and I'm not a target."

"Then I'm going with you."

"I expected that. You're a difficult lady for a man to protect. Why not let me fight this particular dragon?"

She fell into step with him. "He's not a dragon; he's a rat. And, thanks, to my many ventures into subterranean Tamrovia, I've become very familiar with the breed lately. Who knows? I may be able to handle him better than you."

"Naldona is—"

"I'm going with you."

They had reached the head of the staircase. "It appears you already have." Sandor raised his voice. "I'm here, Naldona. Say what you have to say and keep the lights turned out."

"How cautious you are, Sandor." Naldona sounded almost hearty. He had discarded the megaphone, but his voice carried clearly in the high-ceilinged hall. "I told you I had plans for you. I wanted to see your face when I told you about them. I have only a few men down here with me. Surely a legend like the Tanzar can't be afraid."

"I've been enough of a fool for one night," Sandor said dryly. "I'm not about to walk right into your hands, Marc."

"But you've already done that. I have a troop of soldiers at every entrance to the castle, with orders to shoot you on sight." Naldona paused. "Along with the lovely Miss Ballard. Are you there, Miss Ballard?"

"I'm here."

"I wondered how a mere woman was able to evade one of my best men. I should have known Karpathan was involved. It was very discourteous of you to violate my hospitality by departing without saying good-bye. I've had a good deal of trouble reassuring Bruner of my good intentions, and I'm very annoyed with you."

Mere woman? "I thought the assassin you sent to my room would make my explanations," Alessandra said through clenched teeth.

"Oh, he did. He was very eager to make excuses. Unfortunately, it didn't prevent his eventual demise. I was very angry that morning." His tone became silky. "But I'm not angry now. I couldn't be more pleased about the way things are working out. Lovers should share the same fate. It's so very poetic."

She could feel Sandor stiffen next to her. "Lovers?"

"Oh, yes, I know about that. It was really to be expected. The dashing, romantic Tanzar and the whore of—"

"Shut up, Naldona." Sandor's words cut him off with barely restrained violence. "Leave her out of it."

"So gallant. I suppose that's to be expected too. You must forgive me. You can't expect me to have the same sense of delicacy as you. I'm only a poor peasant, while you're a nobleman."

"I believe when we started out together we planned to eliminate that distinction."

"I was an idealistic idiot then, but I soon came to my senses." Naldona laughed. "However, you never did realize what we had in our hands. You've been a fool in more ways than one, Sandor."

"Perhaps." Sandor's voice had regained its coolness. "I'm particularly interested in identifying one aspect of my stupidity. I thought we'd made it into the castle unseen. How did you know we were here?"

"You were unseen. I was a little upset that the guards had grown so careless. I suppose, after all this time, they thought it unlikely you would come back here." Naldona paused. "But I knew you'd come. I knew how you felt about this heap of stone. I would have been even more upset, however, if the guards had failed to pick up your voices on the monitors."

"Monitors?"

"I took the precaution of having the halls of the castle very thoroughly bugged. Both your voice and Miss Ballard's came over very clearly as you were giving her a tour of the ancestral home. My men called me at once in Belajo and requested instructions. I told them to wait until I could get here before they interrupted you in your romantic idyll. Wasn't that kind of me?"

"Very kind," Sandor said. "But I'm sure you had your reasons."

"Oh, I did." Naldona gave a low order, and there was suddenly the sound of rapid footsteps on the parquet floor of the foyer. "Don't be alarmed. My men aren't going to rush you. They're just going to the other rooms on this floor to carry out an order. I think you can imagine what that order is, Sandor."

"Yes." Sandor's voice was harsh with pain. "I can imagine."

"Oh, it hurts, does it? I do wish I could see your face. Can you smell it? The odor is very strong down here."

"No, I can't smell it."

"You will soon. I promise you."

"Sandor?" Alessandra drew a step nearer. "What's happening?"

Naldona's tone held malicious pleasure. "Yes, tell her what's happening, Sandor. Since she's going to suffer a tragic end, she should know the details."

"Did you consider how difficult it will be to explain Alessandra's death to Bruner?"

"I'll find some way of casting the blame on you. Your death will give me considerably more time, Sandor. Your followers will be devastated and thrown into confusion. With Bruner's weapons I'll be able to turn this war around."

"It won't be that easy. I've trained men to take my place."

"But you're the legend, and when a legend dies . . ." There was the sound of footsteps in the foyer again. "It seems we're ready. You have your choice. You'll be blown apart if you try to leave by any of the entrances."

"I know my choice."

"Good. I'm leaving now." There was a sound of a door opening. "But I'll be outside watching. If it lasts all night, I'll still be there, and enjoying every minute of it. I want you to know that."

Sandor didn't answer.

"I do wish I could see your face." Naldona's tone was wistful. A tiny flame flickered in the doorway. A match. "Good-bye, Sandor." The tiny flame plummeted toward a dark, shining pool on the floor.

The pool exploded, sending flames leaping high! The front door closed behind Naldona. Flames were streaking across the foyer, eating everything in their paths and gaining strength as their hunger was fed.

"Gasoline!" Alessandra breathed. "Oh, Lord, he's set fire to the castle."

"Yes." Sandor's face was expressionless as he stared down at the inferno below.

"Can we stop it?"

"No." He stood there an instant more. "Naldona can be very thorough." He turned away. "It's not safe to speak. I imagine Naldona is listening to us right now. He'd love to hear us whimper. He's not going to do that." He took her elbow and turned on the flashlight. "Come on." He was half running down the corridor toward the back staircase leading to the nursery.

"Sandor, can't we—"

He shook his head and touched his fingers to

his lips. Then they were running up the flight of steps of the back staircase. It was only after the door of the nursery closed behind them that he spoke. "I think it's safe to speak in here. Naldona said the listening devices were in the halls, and he evidently didn't know how we entered the castle." He swiftly crossed the room to the panel of the secret passage. "After the first flight of stairs, the secret passage angles away from the castle to the hill. With all Naldona's forces gathered on the castle grounds, there should be no problem getting out unseen through the exit on the hill. The castle should burn for hours, and we'll be at the airfield before Naldona will be able to enter the ruins and search for our remains."

Ruins. This home Sandor loved so much was being destroyed. Alessandra stood watching him as he began to tug at the panel closure, and felt a surge of wild anger. They had no right to do this to him. He had been so happy showing her the house and the objects he loved. He was *good*. He wanted only what was best for his country and his people, and Naldona was doing this monstrous thing to hurt him. She was experiencing the same frustrating despair she had known when Dimitri was dying and she hadn't been able to help him.

Now Limtana was dying and she couldn't do anything to help Sandor either. Well, she couldn't stand here and do nothing. Not this time.

"Damn, this panel is stuck again." Sandor's voice was harsh with impatience. The panel had opened only a few inches. "We'll be lucky if the smoke doesn't begin pouring in on us before I can get it open." He glanced over his shoulder as he heard the door of the nursery open behind him. "Where the hell do you think you're going?"

"Keep working on it. I'll be right back." She heard him call her name, but ignored it as she quickly ran from the nursery and down the back stairs.

Eight

There was already the faintest drift of smoke rising to the second floor. At the other end of the hall Alessandra could see an orange glare reflected from the blazing foyer. It sent a chill through her. That other fire had been like this, merely a reflection at first, then alive and hungry like a beast clawing at— She blocked the thought swiftly. Not now. Never. It was gone. There was only now.

It was too late to go downstairs. She had only a few precious minutes. What pieces had Sandor said the family valued most? The vase on the hall table. It had been a gift from his father to his mother. The snuffbox beside it had a cameo picture of his grandfather inside the lid. The triptych given to his great-grandfather by Czar Nicholas. What else? Oh, Lord, the *casimar*!

She flew down the hall and into the master bedroom. The lovely silk shawl was lying on the chair beside the bed, where Sandor had tossed it.

She snatched it up and bolted from the room. The smoke was thick now, and she had to struggle not to cough. She spread the shawl on the hall table and placed the vase, snuffbox, and triptych in the center and tied the corners into a make-shift knapsack. Her eyes were stinging, and she couldn't repress the coughing now. Her lungs felt seared. She slung the knapsack over her arm and ran toward the back staircase. She had almost reached the top of the steps when Sandor opened the nursery door.

"I was just coming for you. Why did you—?" He broke off as he caught sight of the silk shawl. "You went back for a *shawl*?"

"Among other things." She came into the room and closed the door. "I see you've managed to budge the panel." She looked critically at the dark opening. "We'll need to widen it a few more inches."

"It's wide enough for us to slip through."

"But not wide enough for Leo." She knelt in front of the rocking horse and began to slip the loop of the shawl knapsack from around her arm. "We're taking him with us."

"What?" He was staring at her as if she had gone mad. "He's made of oak and must weigh forty pounds. Besides the stairs and over a mile of passageway, we have three miles of rough hill country to cross before we get to the airfield."

"That's only twenty pounds apiece. We're both tall and strong." She knotted the shawl firmly around the neck of the rocking horse. "I'm not going without him."

"Alessandra—"

"No!" She turned to look at him, her eyes blazing. "He's important. I'm not leaving him for Naldona to destroy. Open the panel wider."

Clearly he was frustrated with her, impatient . . . and feeling some other, more gentle emotion as well. "Oh, hell!" He crossed the room and began tugging at the panel.

She stayed where she was, kneeling in front of the rocking horse. His bright black eyes were gazing at her with eagerness about the adventure to come. "I'm afraid we're going to have to find you a new home, boy," she whispered. "There will never be another *casimar* here, but you'll be all right. You're a survivor, just like me."

The panel finally slid back with a protesting creak. Alessandra looked up. "That should do it." She stood up. "We can go now."

"Thank you." Sandor's tone was ironic and his expression as he looked at the rocking horse completely shuttered. "I think it's time, since smoke is beginning to curl under the door. This is stupid, you know. Are you sure you won't change your mind?"

"No. Do you want the rear end or the front?"

"I'll take the hindquarters. They're heavier." He smiled mirthlessly. "And it's certainly appropriate. I'm being a complete ass for letting you bulldoze me into doing this." He handed her the flashlight. "Fasten this to Leo's knapsack. We'll have to have some light to negotiate those stairs. Ready?"

She nodded as she finished tying the flashlight to the shawl. "Ready."

The journey was just as cumbersome and taxing as Sandor had predicted. Their pace was excruciatingly slow down the flight of steps from the nursery. By the time they had reached the second level they had to be careful not to touch the hot stone wall separating the passage from the castle. Alessandra could imagine what the fire was now doing to the gracious bedroom where she had slept so peacefully only a short time ago. Here and there, wisps of smoke escaped through cracks in the stone to curl around them like ghostly serpents and remind them what lay behind.

The first level was even worse. The passage here was full of smoke, and Alessandra was coughing so hard from that and the strain of carrying the rocking horse, she wove down the last few steps as if she were drunk.

"Put the damn thing down." Sandor was coughing, too, and the harshness of the order was magnified by his hoarseness. "This horse is slowing us down too much. You need to get out of this smoke."

"No, you said it would be better when the passage angled away from the castle. We'll be able to hurry once we've gotten to the bottom of these stairs. I didn't remember there being this many steps."

"Eighty-three," he said grimly. "I counted them once when I was a boy. Alessandra—"

"I can't talk to you now." It was true. It was difficult to breathe, much less talk. "Hurry."

She heard a curse from the direction of Leo's hindquarters.

Then they had finally reached the bottom of the steps opposite the dungeon, and the smoke was thinning out. "See, I told you we'd make it." Her steps quickened as she turned the corner of the passage that angled away from the castle. "We're practically home free."

"Hardly. Tell me that when we're lugging Leo *up*

the steps. Would you like me to tell you how many steps there are between here and the top of the hill?"

She shook her head. "I think I'd rather be surprised." Her arms were aching and the muscles of her legs felt leaden. Close it out. One step at a time. "I like surprises."

There was a short silence behind her. "Do you, love? I'll remember that." His voice lost its softness and became crisp as he continued. "Anytime you decide you want to get rid of our burden, just tell me."

"We can't abandon him. We'll make it."

They did make it, though by the time they had hauled Leo up the final few steps Alessandra had her doubts. The strain on their lungs and muscles was almost unbearable. When she shouldered open the trapdoor and backed out of the tunnel, the fresh night air was a cool blessing on her face.

Sandor stumbled out after her and set his end of the rocking horse on firm ground. "You can let him go now."

"Can I?" She wasn't so sure. Her hands were stiff and sore from clutching the oak runners and, at first, refused to release them. She had to open and close her hands several times after she had set Leo down, before they felt as if they belonged to her again. "You're right, I can." She collapsed on the ground and closed her eyes. "*Now* you can tell me how many steps there were."

"One thousand three hundred and forty-two." He closed the trapdoor and leaned back against the large boulder hiding the passage. "If I remember correctly."

"Oh, I'm sure you remember correctly." She drew

a long, deep breath. Her lungs still hurt, but the fresh air was soothing them more with each passing second. "There were at least that many."

"We don't have to take Leo with us to the airfield. We could hide him in the shrubbery and retrieve him later."

She shook her head without opening her eyes. "It's not safe. No telling what might happen to. him. There's a war going on."

"So I've been told." There was a thread of pain running through the words, and she opened her eyes, expecting to see it echoed in his expression. No pain, His face was as shuttered as it had been when he'd first seen the foyer burst into flame. "We'd better be on our way. Are you ready to go?"

"Yes." She sat up. "I'm ready."

He stood up and flicked off the flashlight, still gleaming in the shawl looped around Leo's neck. "We won't need this light to give our positions away. We'll be—" He broke off as his eyes lifted past the high mound of rocks. *"My God!"*

She knew what he must be seeing, but she had to try to share the agony he was feeling. She stood up and moved a step closer in silent support as her gaze followed his to the valley below.

Limtana was still there. Its massive stone walls were bravely withstanding the flames, as they had the centuries, but every window and opening revealed the harsh orange glare of the cannibal flames devouring it from within. Sparks had ignited a bush and two trees in the garden, and they were being destroyed by the same hungry beast. And Naldona was down there watching it happen. The anger and despair that exploded in Alessandra were titanic. Oh, damn. *Damn.* She wasn't aware of the tears running down her cheeks, until she felt Sandor's fingers gently tracing their path.

"For me?"

"For you. For Limtana. For me." She fell to her knees again beside Leo. "It's all so futile to save Leo and the *casimar* and have you lose Limtana. Lose it completely. I failed again. I had to stand by and let them take—"

"You didn't fail." His gaze was still on the destruction below.

"It was my fault." Her arms encircled the neck of the rocking horse, and she buried her face in his painted mane like a bereaved child seeking comfort. "You wouldn't have stopped if it hadn't been for me. This wouldn't have happened."

"It would have happened."

"No, you wouldn't have stopped. My stupid feet . . ."

She was in pain. She was crying for his loss. He had to try to jerk himself out of this numbness he had deliberately placed on his emotions and help her. Tears would never come easily for Alessandra. Lord, but he didn't want to begin to feel again right now. Not yet. Not when he could still see Limtana burning. He closed his eyes. Think about Alessandra. Think about life, the future. Don't think about gaping windows filled with licking flames. Don't. . . .

He opened his eyes and slowly knelt down beside her. Her face was still burrowed against the rocking horse, and he began to stroke her hair. "It's all right. None of this is your fault. If it hadn't happened tonight, there would have been another night. I knew it was only a question of time."

"You *knew* Naldona would burn Limtana?"

He nodded, his hand moving over her hair with infinite gentleness. "When Naldona sent me the picture of Limtana, he made it very clear that no matter how the war turned out, I'd never have my home again. He said his first move when he knew he was defeated would be to burn Limtana to the ground."

But Sandor could have saved Limtana. He had told her his forces had the ability to take this strip of land that held the home he loved. He'd had the power to issue that order and he hadn't used the power. "Why? Why didn't you save it?"

"I didn't have the right," he said simply. "I told you, Limtana has no strategic importance."

But Limtana had been of monumental importance to him. She didn't know whether she would have been able to make the same sacrifice if she had known she could save something she loved merely by lifting a finger. She felt a wrenching pain at the thought of what he must have gone through. Strength. Her first impression had been of the field of strength surrounding Sandor, but she'd had no idea how strong he really was.

His expression was no longer guarded, and she could see the lines of pain etched in his face. And he had been trying to comfort *her*! "I'm sorry. I know there aren't any words that will help, but I'm so very sorry, Sandor."

"I know you are." His lips twisted as his gaze returned to the scene in the valley. "I don't know. Maybe I needed to lose something I loved to the war. You were right when you said that I had less to lose than others. Maybe this is some kind of macabre justice."

"No, I never should have said it. I didn't know . . ." She hadn't known how good he was or how much he cared. She hadn't known so many things about him. "There's no justice about this. I'd like to *strangle* Naldona."

A faint smile touched his lips. "You'd have to stand in a long line." He slowly shook his head. "But not for this. Memories are more important than possessions. He can't destroy my memories. That's the reason I brought you here tonight. I wanted to have the memory of you here at the place I loved the most. It meant a great deal to me."

The tears were falling again. She couldn't seem to stop now. She hadn't cried when Dimitri died. Her conflicting emotions—rage predominating—had prevented tears. "Sandor . . ." She suddenly straightened and threw herself into his arms. "Hold me." She didn't want him to be alone. She didn't know if physical touch would help to soothe his pain, but it was all she had to give. "It will be all right. I'll make it be all right."

His hands cradled her head, her fingers tangling in her hair. "How fierce you are." His lips brushed her temple. "We should be leaving now, you know."

"A few minutes more won't matter." She held him tight, trying to communicate all the strength, sympathy, and love she felt for him. Love. Why had she been so afraid to acknowledge it? There was nothing to fear in loving Sandor. "Let me help you. Let me *give* to you."

"Pity?"

"No, I didn't mean—"

"Shh. It's all right." He was rocking her gently.

"I'm not too proud to accept pity. It's all a part of any decent human relationship to want to help the people we care about and to feel sympathy when they're in trouble."

"I do want to help." The words were muffled against his shoulder. "Please tell me what I can do to help you."

"You are helping." His voice was husky. It was true. The first raw pain was easing. His arms tightened around her. "You are helping, love."

They didn't speak again. The only sound in the forest was the breeze rustling through the pines and the distant crackling roar in the valley below. They knelt there, holding each other, while the rocking horse's bright painted eyes gazed blindly toward the horizon.

"It's not exactly . . . large, is it?" Alessandra asked as she gazed at the airfield enclosed by the ten-foot barbed-wire fence. "I guess I was expecting something the size of LaGuardia."

"It's big enough. It has three runways long enough to accommodate jets." He laughed softly. "This is Tamrovia, remember?"

"How could I forget? I feel as if I've walked over three fourths of the hallowed ground of your sovereign state."

"I imagine you do. Can I convince you it's safe to put Leo down now? I promise I'll have someone from the field drive out and pick him up as soon as we pass the gates."

"I guess so." She carefully set the rocking horse down in the grass at the side of the road and straightened with a sigh of relief. "I was beginning to feel as if he were permanently attached to me." She frowned. "Are you sure he'll be all right?"

"Positive." He smiled gently. "After all you've suffered for him, I wouldn't dare let anything happen to Leo. How are your feet?"

"Sore." She rubbed the nape of her neck wearily. "I'll survive."

"I've noticed you make a habit of doing that." His smile faded. "I haven't taken very good care of you. I promise I'll do better. When this is all over, I promise you won't have to walk a step."

"The way I feel at the moment, I'd probably hold you to that promise. Just how do you intend to fulfill it? I refuse to be relegated to a wheelchair."

"I was thinking of something more on the order of a ricksha." Sandor's eyes were suddenly twinkling. "A very special ricksha, with wheels of gold and the spokes set with jade and amber. I believe you'd look quite regal in such a ricksha, Alessandra."

"Pulled by a majordomo in a scarlet uniform with gold braid?"

"If milady desires." He bowed.

She made a face. "The only thing milady desires right now is a bath and a bed. And since there's no ricksha available, I guess I'll have to force these feet to move. Not that I—"

"I congratulate you. For ghosts, you look in magnificent health."

She jumped. then she relaxed as she recognized the big man who had seemingly materialized out of the trees. "Paulo, what on earth are you doing here?"

"Looking for you. I'm glad to see Naldona's announcement on his broadcast was exaggerated."

"Broadcast?" Sandor frowned. "What broadcast?"

"The one he made announcing your death, along with that of your 'brutalized captive,' Alessandra Ballard." He tilted his head and appraised her critically. "You don't appear brutalized—a little tired, maybe." His dark eyes twinkled. "But we all know how expert Sandor is at torture. No doubt the fiend could brutalize you without leaving a single mark."

"When?" Sandor asked tersely.

"The broadcast? Thirty minutes ago. Conal radioed the airfield from the base and asked me to go to Limtana and verify the report. I was just setting out when I saw you approaching the airfield." Paulo's teeth flashed in his bearded face. "Conal was very worried he might have to step into your shoes. He will be extremely relieved to know that won't be necessary."

'Not as relieved as I am," Sandor said dryly. "What are you doing at the airfield?"

"Waiting for you. You certainly tend to become distracted from your objectives when you're with Miss Ballard. I started at noon yesterday and arrived at the airfield last night. I was surprised to find you hadn't arrived yet. Then, when Conal heard the broadcast, he—"

"Why were you waiting for me?" Sandor said incisively. "And why did you follow us?"

Paulo grinned. "Good news. We received a message from Zack. He managed to untangle the problem with the delivery. The arms were delivered to the base last night. Conal didn't want to risk a radio leak to tip Naldona to the fact that the assault was imminent, so he sent me to tell you and bring you back."

"I'll say it's good news." Sandor's eyes blazed, the weariness falling away from him. "Lord, it's almost over. I've got to contact Conal and . . ." His voice trailed off, and he strode toward the high fence bordering the airfield. He glanced back over his shoulder, shouting, "Take care of her, Paulo."

Alessandra slowly shook her head as she watched him walk away. She supposed she should be grateful he had even remembered her existence. He had closed her out again. "Yes, take care of me, Paulo," she said ironically. "But be sure I don't get in the way."

"The war is—"

She held up her hand. "I know. I'm not criticizing your Tanzar's dedication. Priorities have to be observed. I just don't like being put on a shelf and expected to stay there." They had shared so much in the last hours that she hadn't expected this rejection. "I think Sandor and I will have to discuss a few things. Now, do you suppose you could manage to find me a bath and a place to sleep for the next few hours?"

"The bath is easy. A place to sleep may be impossible. Once Sandor begins to move, there won't be a quiet room or spot on the entire airfield." He shrugged. "Maybe not in all Tamrovia . . . but I will try. If anyone can do it—"

"It will be you," Alessandra finished. "I have complete faith in your ingenuity, Paulo." She adjusted the straps of her backpack and brushed the hair from her temple. "Shall we go and put it to the test?"

"Do you want to take our friend, here?" Paulo gestured to the rocking horse. His lips were twitching with amusement. "I was going to question Sandor about it, when he ran off." He lowered his voice. "What is it? A new secret weapon?"

"His name is Leo," she said, and sighed. "And yes, I think we'd better take him with us." If Paulo was right about the coming turmoil, there was no telling when anyone from the airfield would be free to come and pick him up. She bent to grasp the the oak runners. "You take the hindquarters."

It was done. The arms were distributed and in place. Conal and Jasper would be on their way within the hour to position their troops for the rear attack on Belajo. He had only to fly back to base to join his men and take command of the frontal attack.

Sandor leaned back in the chair and gazed at the radio he had just switched off. He should be tired, but adrenaline was charging him with vitality. He hoped to heaven it lasted. A long forty-eight hours loomed ahead for him. Forty-eight hours. After two long years, it was almost over. He would be able to stop thinking of war and begin thinking of—

"Your helicopter is ready." Paulo stood in the doorway of the radio room. "I'm surprised you decided to go by air. What about Naldona's anti-aircraft guns?"

"They'll be taken out. Conal has sent troops to take care of it. A foray toward Limtana will act as a diversion to keep Naldona from noticing we're shifting our forces to encircle Belajo. If we move quickly, we'll take him off guard. He thought the news of my death would throw our forces into confusion." His lips twisted. "His men are probably still sifting through the ashes for our remains. The damage to Limtana must have been pretty close to total for him to risk the announcement without concrete proof."

Paulo's expression was grave. "I am sorry about your home. I know how highly you valued it. I cannot understand this passion for a single dwelling, but I share your grief." He grinned. "Perhaps it is for the best. Who knows? Maybe when you have won this war, you will join my tribe and we'll show you how a man should live. No walls, no roots, no politics."

"No politics." Sandor grimaced. "That alone makes your invitation irresistible."

"We will hide you in the hills. If they can't find you, they can't make you president."

"Well, I'll worry about that when we've gotten rid of Naldona." He pushed back his chair. "I have to see Alessandra before I leave. Where is she?"

"In the machine shed."

"The machine shed?"

"She wanted to take a nap. It was the only place I could put her where your people wouldn't be stumbling over her. I put a cot in there and found her a pair of earplugs." Paulo's expression reflected satisfaction. "It worked very well. When I checked on her thirty minutes ago, she didn't even stir."

"After what we've been through in the past two days, it wouldn't surprise me if she slept for a month. Meet me at the helicopter in fifteen minutes, will you? There's something I want you to do for me."

The machine shed smelled of oil and the concrete floor was stained with grease and spotted with paint. Alessandra was totally unaware of either the odor or the roughness of her surroundings. She was breathing deeply, evenly, sleeping the sleep of total exhaustion.

Sandor knelt beside her. He didn't have much time, but he wanted to spend these last minutes with her. There were a hundred things he still had to say to her. Their time together had been pitifully brief and shadowed by violence and misunderstanding. His glance fell on the rocking horse someone had shoved into the far corner of the shed. He hadn't even told her how much it had meant, how much it had touched him, to have her fight so valiantly to preserve a part of his heritage. How could he hope she'd realize what they'd found together? He'd have to *make* her understand. When this miserable war was over, he'd find her and convince her he could be something other than the rough soldier she had known these last few days.

He reached out his hand to touch her cheek. He stopped in midair and let his hand fall to his side without touching her. He had forgotten the wariness that was always with her. If he touched her, he would wake her, and he didn't want to. He hoped she slept until all the horror of the coming attack was in the past. She had gone through one war. He would not inflict another on her. He would just stay here until it was time for him to leave. He would think about last night and the possibility of tomorrow. It would be enough.

Nine

There was something wrong.

Alessandra's eyes flew open, instinctive alarm jarring her awake. It was dark. The rancid odor of oil was heavy in the air. The machine shed. She remembered now. Paulo had found her a place to sleep for a few hours. . . . But that had been mid-morning, and it was dark now. She sat bolt upright and fumbled to remove her earplugs. Why hadn't someone awakened her?

Something was stirring across the room. She jerked around to face it.

"It's only me." Paulo's voice. "Don't be afraid." A match suddenly flared in the darkness, illuminating Paulo's bearded face and sparkling eyes. "Sandor asked me to watch over you. I'm glad you're awake. I was getting restless sitting here." The match was extinguished and she heard a rustling as Paulo rose to his feet and moved across the room toward the light switch. "You slept a long time. Sandor said you were exhausted."

Alessandra blinked as Paulo switched on the harsh overhead light. She swung her feet to the floor. "What time is it?"

"Three in the morning." He shrugged. "Maybe later."

It was the middle of the night. For a moment she couldn't take it in. "Why didn't somebody wake me? Where's Sandor?"

"Gone back to the base."

"Without me? He *left* me here?"

Paulo nodded, not looking at her. "He said it would be safer for you. He's radioed Zack to send a jet to take you to Zurich. He told me to tell you he'd join you as soon as he could."

Alessandra stared at him blankly. "I'm to go to Switzerland and he'll join me when it's convenient?"

Paulo nodded. "It shouldn't be too long. Sandor has already launched the attack on Belajo. They should be in the thick of the fighting right now."

Fighting. Sandor was surrounded by violence and death and she wasn't with him. He could die and she wouldn't even know it. And he wanted her to go to Switzerland? "How do I get to Belajo?"

Paulo smiled in satisfaction. "It's very dangerous," he murmured. "And difficult. Sandor will be angry."

"How do I get there?"

"Fighting is fierce around Limtana, and we have to cross that territory to get to Belajo."

"*How,* Paulo?"

"We walk."

She made a face. "I was afraid of that."

"It will be very interesting. I know many ways to avoid—"

"I'm sure you do, and none of them in a straight line. It will probably take us twice as long as the trip coming here."

"Possibly. You do not like to walk?"

"Let's just say walking doesn't like me."

Paulo's eyes were innocent. "You could stay here or go to Zurich. I'm certain you'd be very comfortable at either place."

"We walk."

He threw back his head and laughed. "I thought you would. That's why I didn't argue with Sandor when he asked me to stay. I knew that you and I would have a better time together than I would have had with him in Belajo. Battle takes little skill. It is the hunt that challenges a man. Whether he's the prey or the hunter, it is the hunt."

She found herself smiling. He was like a zestful child, and his enthusiasm was contagious. Paulo and Leo would have made a fine pair, she thought with amusement. The adventure just over the horizon beckoned to both of them. She felt a tiny thrill of anticipation herself as she started for the door. "Let's hope the challenges aren't too extreme this time. Let me wash up and get something to eat and we'll be on our way."

Belajo was a madhouse of joy. Singing, dancing in the streets, cafés giving out free wine and ale. Paulo had to step in twice before they had gone four blocks from the city gates to keep Alessandra from being swept away by a wave of enthusiastic merrymakers.

"Perhaps we had better go down one of the side streets," he suggested, his big hand holding firmly to her wrist to keep her at his side. "Victory has a way of causing a certain amount of madness. A pleasant madness. It is good to see the people so happy. They suffered much under Naldona, and Sandor is extremely popular."

"That's very obvious." She had heard many shouts of "Karpathan!" and "Tanzar!" since she had entered the city. "Is it really over?"

"So it seems." Paulo shrugged. "I will know more when we run across one of Sandor's officers. The city is secure and we had little trouble crossing Limtana. Sandor's army evidently made a clean sweep."

"But where can we find Sandor? The palace?"

"Possibly." He frowned. "You look very tired. Sandor will not be pleased. Why don't you sit down at that outdoor café across the street, and I will find Sandor and bring him to you."

It was tempting. The last twenty-four hours had been a nightmare of pain and exhaustion. The trip through the hills might have been an interesting exercise in evasion for Paulo, but for her it had been fraught with agony and worry. She hadn't been certain Sandor was safe, until they ran into a troop of soldiers outside the city who told them of Sandor's victory. Now all she had to worry about was finding Sandor in a city gone crazy with excitement, and trying to stay upright on feet that felt as if they'd been slashed by the knives of Sandor's mermaid story. She shook her head. "No. I've come this far, and there's no telling how long it will take you to find Sandor."

"You have great strength. Are you sure you aren't a gypsy?"

"I'm not sure of anything. There are—"

"Ho! Conal!" Paulo's shout interrupted her. He released her wrist. "Wait here." He agilely dodged his way through the crowd toward a canvas-covered truck carrying soldiers that was slowly negotiating its way through the streets. "Stop, Conal!"

The truck stopped and the passenger door of the cab opened. The dark, stocky man who leaned out to speak to Paulo looked vaguely familiar, Alessandra thought. She'd probably seen him at the base. She stepped back into the alcove of a butcher shop to get out of the crowd and leaned wearily against the wall.

Paulo and the soldier spoke for only a few minutes, and then Paulo was cutting his way through the crowd toward her.

"Well?"

"It's not good." Paulo's expression was grave. "We've won the war, but Naldona refuses to surrender. His personal guard has barricaded his suite at the palace, and he has a hostage." He paused. "James Bruner."

"James!" She straightened. "But he has nothing to do with this."

"He's an American citizen. If anything happens to him, the United States government will be very upset. A brand-new republic can't afford to annoy a superpower."

"But nothing could happen to James. He doesn't—" She broke off. As long as James was held by Naldona, anything was possible. "You said he was a hostage. What does Naldona want?"

"A helicopter to take him to the airport. A jet to

take him where he wishes to go from there." He hesitated. "And Sandor Karpathan."

A tingle of shock ran through her. "Sandor couldn't give into a demand like that. Naldona would kill him. His men wouldn't *let* him do it."

"Sandor is the Tanzar. His men will do as he commands."

"No!" She drew a shuddering breath. Surely Sandor wouldn't do it. Yet who knew better than she how much he had already given up? Why had she and James even come to Tamrovia? It was her fault both James and Sandor were in danger, and it was her responsibility to correct that situation. "Where is Sandor now?"

"He is at the palace. His men have set up a position in the courtyard. Naldona has given him another six hours to make a decision before he kills Bruner."

Six hours. She felt a surge of relief so great, her legs went weak. At least Sandor would be safe until she had time to figure out what to do. "Oh, thank God."

"Conal is waiting in the truck to take us to the palace. Sandor has sent for more troops. I thought you would want to go with him."

"Yes." She spoke abstractedly as she began to wend her way through the crowd. "Yes, I want to go the palace." The secret passage! She skidded to a stop. If Sandor didn't put himself in Naldona's hands, it was almost certain he would use the secret passage for a surprise attack. The action would put him right in Naldona's lap. But even if Naldona was surprised, it didn't mean there wouldn't be violence. James or Sandor still could be either hurt or ki— She mustn't think about what might happen. She had to decide what to do. What were Naldona's weak points? There must be something she could use. Women. His attitude toward women was—

"Alessandra?" Paulo was gazing at her in puzzlement.

She began walking quickly, almost running, toward the truck. "I need a weapon, Paulo. Something that can be easily hidden."

"A weapon," Paulo repeated slowly. "Now, I wonder why you need a weapon?"

"This is my fault. I'm the one who has to straighten it out. Sandor could be killed . . ."

"You are going after Bruner yourself." Paulo's gaze was narrowed on her face. "The secret passage?"

Her eyes widened in surprise. "You know about the passage?"

He nodded. "I met Sandor for the first time in that passage. It was a very interesting evening." He was silent for a moment. "I will go with you."

"No, I can't have anyone along who might make Naldona suspicious. I've decided to try to play on Naldona's contempt for my sex. Judging by that flea-brained mistress he keeps, it's probable he thinks we have only one skill worth cultivating." She smiled crookedly. "I have to appear just as flea-brained and vulnerable. You have to admit you're not exactly unintimidating."

"Who, me?" His teeth were bared in a wolfish grin. "I'm as gentle as a pussycat."

"Well, I don't need a pussycat. I need a weapon."

"You can't go alone. You are the Tanzar's woman. You would be a more valuable hostage for Naldona than Bruner."

"I'm not the Tanzar's woman. I'm my own woman. But if Naldona thinks I'm Sandor's plaything, so much the better. He won't have his guard up."

"I don't know . . ."

"It's the only way there's even a chance of there being no casualties." Her voice held a hint of desperation. "Don't argue with me, Paulo. Help me."

Paulo's gaze was fixed on her thoughtfully. "You will go anyway, won't you?"

She nodded.

"Then I will help you. What kind of weapon?"

A miniscule amount of the tension left her. "A small gun, preferably. I hate knives."

"We will see what Conal can find in the truck. Among an entire troop, surely we'll be able to find one small gun for the Tanzar's woman."

"I'm not—" She stopped. What did it matter what he called her? Perhaps she was Sandor's woman. If love was the common denominator of possession, then Sandor was certainly her man. "Sandor mustn't know about this."

He shook his head. "I can't promise. All I can guarantee is that you'll have a head start. It will be up to you to make the most of it. Conal is very devoted to Sandor, and I won't be able to keep him quiet for long."

"I'll make the most of it. Thank you, Paulo."

"You don't have to thank me. I would not let you go if I didn't think you had a chance. As I said, you are a strong woman." He smiled. "There are times when you remind me of my sister, Marna."

"You have a sister here in Tamrovia?"

"No, she and my tribe are in the United States

right now. Zack Damon found them a fine, free place to stay until the end of the war."

"But you didn't go with them?"

"The hunting was better here. But now that Sandor has won his war, it may become very boring. Perhaps I will go to this Montana."

"The war's not over yet." Not while Naldona was still threatening Sandor and James. Not yet. But it would be over soon, if she had anything to say about it.

She had reached the cab of the truck, and took Conal's hand and let him pull her onto the seat next to him. "I don't think we were introduced at the base." She smiled at him with dazzling sweetness. "I'm Alessandra Ballard, the Tanzar's woman, and I was wondering if you would do me a great favor."

Alessandra turned the sconce, and the bookshelf panel swiveled open. She stood there in the passage, hesitating. No voices. She gave a sigh of relief. She had thought Naldona would take James to his own suite instead of setting up his headquarters here, but there was no way of being sure. She stepped into the sitting room and turned the sconce on the wall to close the panel. So far, so good. The suite appeared to be empty. She moved silently toward her bedroom. She didn't have much time, but she couldn't convince Naldona she was a helpless sex toy while she looked more like a soldier.

It took less than four minutes to change into a white silk blouse and baggy white slacks that hid the small pistol tied to her calf. She took down her hair and brushed it swiftly. She had no time for makeup. She didn't have to look beautiful, only womanly. Shoes. They had to be totally impractical to blend with the image she needed to create. She stripped off her tennis shoes and socks and thrust her feet into high-heeled sandals. She gasped as her weight was thrown onto the ball of her feet. She closed her eyes and drew a deep breath, waiting for the pain to abate to a point where she could block it out. She opened her eyes. Good heavens, she was pale. She couldn't worry about that now. She turned away from the mirror and walked slowly, carefully out of the bedroom and crossed the sitting room to the door opening into the hall.

She managed to slip unnoticed out of the suite, but had gone only a few yards down the hall toward Naldona's suite when she heard the cocking of a pistol behind her. "Halt!"

"I'm halted, for goodness' sake," she said peevishly. She looked over her shoulder at the soldier holding the gun. "You don't have to threaten me with that thing. I'm frightened enough as it is. Where's Naldona?"

The door to Naldona's suite opened. "Miss Ballard?" Marc Naldona stood in the doorway. "How nice of you to drop in. Would you care to tell me how you managed it? You and Karpathan appear to be escape artists on a par with Houdini."

She waved her hand vaguely. "Sandor showed me a way from the terrace up a back staircase. I was too scared to pay much attention." She scowled. "I don't like being used as a pawn by the two of you. I'm an American citizen, dammit."

"Pawn?" Naldona's dark eyes were narrowed on

her. Cold eyes. "Why do you think Karpathan would use you as a pawn? He was quite defensive of you at Limtana."

"That was before you burned his bloody castle. You would have thought that damn pile of wood and stone was alive. He turned into a raving maniac."

"Really?" There was a flicker of savage satisfaction in Naldona's face. "He was hurting?"

Damn him. She could almost feel the pleasure radiating from the bastard. She lowered her lashes to veil her eyes. "Bleeding. He went wild. Cursing you." She inserted a thread of indignation into her tone. "He even blamed me. What did I have to do with it? I couldn't help it if I got too tired to travel anymore that night. He was eager enough to drag me into the nearest bedroom. Now he treats me as if I have leprosy, or something."

"How unfortunate. But that doesn't tell me why Sandor sent you into the lion's den." His lips twisted. "Or why you let yourself be sent."

"Karpathan seemed to think another hostage might pacify you. I was certainly willing to come. James never treated me like Karpathan. James was always very kind to me. When you let him go, I want to go with him. There isn't any reason for you to hurt me now." She gazed at him limpidly. "May I see James?"

He hesitated and then shrugged. "Why not?" He stood aside. "Come in, Miss Ballard, and join the party." He motioned to the guard, who lowered the pistol. "It's too bad you'll be of no use to me with Karpathan, but I still may find a way to improve my situation. Bruner is a very rich man, and I'll need money to make my exile comfortable. He appears to be very fond of you."

"I know how to please a man." Alessandra entered the suite. "James and I understood each other." She glanced anxiously over her shoulder. "You didn't tell him what happened between Karpathan and me?"

He shook his head. "Your little secret is safe for the moment. Perhaps it will remain so if you give me the help I need with Bruner." He nodded to the door of the bedroom. "He's locked in there. He'll be delighted that I've returned his little playmate to him." He reached into his pocket, pulled out a key, and handed it to her. "Show him a good time. If Karpathan doesn't give me what I want, it may be the last one he has."

"You wouldn't do that. We're American citizens." She strode confidently toward the bedroom door. "You and Karpathan will work things out and then James and I will leave here." She unlocked the door. "I've had enough of Tamrovia to last me for the rest of my life."

Naldona strolled to the center of the room. "American citizen. You say it like a magic incantation. It means nothing here."

"Of course it means something here." She tossed her head. Lord, what a phony gesture. Next she'd be neighing like a Shetland pony. "Everyone knows you can't monkey around with Uncle Sam."

"Alessandra!" James was sitting on the bed, and he jumped to his feet.

"Oh, darling, you can't imagine what I've been through." She ran across the room and kissed him on the cheek. "Fires and that horrible Karpathan man and—" She stopped, her gaze searching his face. "You look tired. Are you well? Sit down." She pushed him gently back on the bed and knelt in front of him. "I shouldn't have left you. No one can take care of you the way I can." She smiled brilliantly into his bewildered face while her hand slipped beneath the edge of her baggy trousers to clasp the handle of the pistol. "But now I'm back, and I'll make sure . . ." She drew out the gun with one smooth movement, turned to face Naldona, and finished the sentence. ". . . we both get out of here."

The satisfied smile on Naldona's face vanished. "You're being incredibly stupid. I have thirty men down the hall. One shot and they'll be in this room in seconds."

"That won't do you any good if the bullet is aimed at you. I'm a fair shot, and I won't hesitate to pull the trigger." She rose to her feet and met his gaze steadily. "You have a habit of underestimating people, Naldona. Sandor, James, me. Don't make that mistake now."

He studied her for a moment before slowly shaking his head. "You're an excellent bluffer, but I don't think you're capable of following through on it." His lips curved contemptuously as his gaze moved over her. "You don't learn such strength of purpose in the bedroom. You'd be wiser to stick to whoring."

James stepped impulsively forward. "Naldona, you son of—"

"No, James," Alessandra said quickly. "It doesn't matter." She gestured with the pistol. "We're going for a little walk, Naldona."

"You think I'm going to let you use *me* as a hostage? Absolutely not." Naldona's eyes glared fiercely into her own. "The only way to handle a bluffer is to call the bluff. Your bluff is called, whore." He deliberately turned his back and began to walk toward the door. "I'm going to call the guards. If you give up now, I might let you live."

Choice. Oh, Lord, she didn't want to shoot him. The thought filled her with cold horror. Yet if she didn't, he would call his men and any chance of saving James would be gone. His suspicions would be thoroughly roused and he'd be ready for Sandor's attack force. Sandor and Paulo, and no telling how many others, might be killed or hurt. On the other hand, without a leader, there was a strong possibility Naldona's men would surrender.

"Stop, Naldona. I mean it."

He didn't turn around. "Your voice is shaking. You don't like violence, do you? I enjoy it. I've acquired quite a taste for it over the years. Karpathan probably has too."

"No." But Naldona was speaking the truth concerning himself. He did enjoy violence. The torture squads, Limtana burning in the night. "I don't want to do this, but I will. Don't open that door."

"A bluff," he said. He reached for the knob of the door.

She pulled the trigger.

"I guess you are angry with me, eh?" Paulo straightened, moving away from the boulder against which he'd been leaning as Sandor and his men came pouring into the cave. He glanced reproachfully at Conal, who stood at Sandor's side. "You didn't wait very long before telling him. She's only been gone fifteen minutes."

"Long enough to get killed. If Naldona has hurt her, I'm going to strangle you both." Sandor slipped behind the boulder and into the entrance of the passage. As he turned on his flashlight, his face was pale and more grim than Paulo had ever seen it. "I told you to take care of her. I wanted her out of the country."

"She's a very determined woman. She had a right to make the decision for herself."

Sandor was moving at a half trot through the passage.

Paulo lengthened his stride to keep up with him. "Don't blame Conal. He was willing to try anything to save your neck." He paused. "So was Alessandra."

Sandor's only answer was to quicken his pace.

The first thing they heard when they exited the secret passage into the sitting room was the sound of a shot. The pounding of boots in the hall followed immediately.

"Alessandra." Sandor tore across the sitting room and jerked open the door. "Oh, God, *Alessandra.*"

More shots. Voices lifted in confusion.

The hall was crammed with Naldona's guards milling about, and the door to the dictator's suite was open wide. A man's voice rang out harshly. "He's dead, dammit. You have nothing left to fight for. Naldona's dead. I have to get her to a doctor."

Her? Sandor took a step forward.

Paulo grasped his arm and jerked him back into the sitting room. "You're not thinking. They're like a flock of geese fluttering around a barnyard. You've got to get their attention and show them where the threat lies." He grabbed Conal's machine gun and sprayed a barrage of bullets over the heads of the soldiers in the hall. The confusion doubled as they whirled to face the new attack. "That should do it." Paulo tossed the machine gun back to Conal.

Sandor's soldiers rushed forward, and in minutes Naldona's men had been subdued and Sandor was pushing his way into Naldona's suite. He cast only a cursory glance at Naldona's body, on the floor by the door. His entire attention was fixed on James Bruner and the still, white-clad woman he was kneeling beside. Alessandra.

"Get a doctor," he ordered hoarsely, not taking his eyes off her. "Now." He walked across the room. He felt as if he were moving in slow motion. His voice also sounded distorted and far away to him. "She's been hit?"

Bruner had unbuttoned Alessandra's white blouse and was using his handkerchief to apply pressure to a bleeding wound on her left side. "Yes." He glanced up. "Karpathan?"

Sandor nodded as he dropped to his knees. Lord, she was pale. Her long lashes were dark shadows on her cheeks. "She's unconscious. How bad is it?"

"I have no idea. I'm not a doctor." Bruner's lips twisted. "You never should have let her come after me."

"I didn't let her," Sandor said dully. The blood was slowly seeping through her white blouse. "Where the hell is that doctor?"

"She shot Naldona."

"Did she?" He couldn't have cared less about Naldona at that moment. Sandor reached out to stroke the hair away from her face. His gaze suddenly lifted, his eyes blazing fiercely in his pale face. "Who shot her?"

"I don't know. One of the soldiers who burst in here after she shot Naldona. Does it matter?"

"It matters." Sandor would get great pleasure from punishing the bastard who had hurt Alessandra. But he couldn't do that yet. Now he had to concentrate all his energy on saving her.

"More violence," Bruner said with acid bitterness. "Won't you ever learn? You've nearly killed her. Alessandra hates war and violence, and you've caused her to shoot a man. If she lives, how do you think she's going to feel about that?"

If she lived. She had to live. Sandor didn't think he'd be able to exist without her. "I don't know." His hand resumed its tender stroking motion at her temple. "I just don't know."

Ten

He was falling, crumpling to the floor in slow, slow motion. The shot still echoed in her ears and her eyes and her heart as she watched with sick horror. The gun in her hand was terribly heavy, but she couldn't seem to let it fall. It was stuck to her hand. She didn't want to hold it. She never wanted to touch a gun again. "No. Please, no."

"Shh. It's all right. You're fine now." Sandor's voice. Sandor's hand holding tightly to her own.

She opened her eyes. "Sandor?" she whispered. "You're safe?"

He was sitting on the bed beside her. His deep blue eyes were glittering. "I'm safe," he said. He cleared his throat. "Bruner's safe. And so are you. The doctor said your wound isn't much more than a scratch. The only reason you fainted was exhaustion." He paused. "And shock."

Shock. Naldona. "Is Naldona . . . ?"

Sandor's hand tightened. "Yes."

She felt the waves of sickness return. "I was afraid he was."

"Dear heaven, don't cry. It's tearing me apart."

She hadn't known she was crying, but now she became aware of the tears running slowly down her cheeks. "I've never had to do that before."

"He was a bloodthirsty bastard." Sandor's voice was harsh. "Everyone in Tamrovia wants to give you a medal. You're a national heroine."

"He was a man." She closed her eyes wearily. "I didn't want to do it, Sandor. I didn't want to hurt anyone."

"I know you didn't. Go back to sleep, love. You'll feel better when you wake up."

"Will I?" She doubted if this terrible depression could be alleviated—much less banished—by sleep. But Sandor had said she would feel better, and it must be true. Sandor wouldn't lie to her. She could trust Sandor. . . .

"I don't want to stay in bed," Alessandra said firmly. "You told me the doctor assured you it was only a very minor flesh wound. I can't lie in this bed any longer. It will drive me up the wall."

James chuckled. "Longer? You only regained consciousness two hours ago. I wouldn't say you've been exactly bedfast. The doctor also said you need rest and relaxation." His smile faded. "And to stay off those feet as much as possible for the next two weeks."

"I can't do that." She sat up in bed, flinching as a hot twinge shot through her side. Why did every muscle in her body ache, when only her left side had been grazed? "I have to see Sandor."

"You can't see him now. He's in a cabinet meeting. We sent a message to let him know you'd finally decided to wake up."

"You shouldn't have let me sleep so long. Thirty-six hours." She shook her head. "It's incredible."

"Not at all. According to Karpathan, you've been driven to the edge of exhaustion. He said the last few days had been a nightmare for you."

Not all of it had been a nightmare. There had been moments of beauty and warmth and passion. Moments she would remember for the rest of her life. Sandor Karpathan had stepped into her life and transfigured it in every way. "Cabinet meeting? That sounds very official."

"As official as anything can be with a fledgling government. Sandor has formed a temporary cabinet to set up committees and act as a governing body until a constitution can be drafted and an election held." He made a face. "I'm surprised the cabinet's wrangling didn't awaken you. Karpathan refused to leave you for the first twenty-four hours, so his cabinet set up shop in the sitting room. It seems they decided they couldn't do without Karpathan. That appears to be the common feeling here in Tamrovia. Everything stops without him."

"Yes." She could endorse that viewpoint. Her own world would stop without Sandor. He had stayed with her during a period when the demands on him must have been titanic. She felt the familiar warm radiance begin deep within her. "They love him."

"And they're not the only ones." James's gaze

was searching her face. "I think you must share the general hysteria. I suppose I should have suspected as much. He was almost out of his mind with worry until the doctor assured him you'd be fine in a few days. It's very rare for that depth of emotion to exist without reciprocation."

"I do love him." The words felt strange and came hesitantly to her lips, but what was there to be hesitant about? He was a man any woman would be proud to love. She lifted her chin. "I'm absolutely mad about Sandor Karpathan."

"Well, you were never one to do things halfway." His hand covered hers on the counterpane of the bed. "Does that mean I'm going to have to go to Mariba alone?"

"We'll work something out. Nothing is settled." She hadn't even told Sandor she loved him. She experienced an instant of uncertainty. For that matter, he had made only the most fleeting mention of any lasting emotion to her. No, there hadn't been any need for words. Sandor had said words weren't always necessary. The bond between them might be new, but it was very strong. "I have to talk to Sandor."

"I believe we've gone over that ground before."

"And I'm *not* staying in bed."

"Alessandra . . ."

"She is causing you trouble?" Paulo stood in the doorway. "Sandor said she would. He also said we are to keep her in bed until he can make arrangements for her."

"Arrangements? I don't need 'arrangements.' All I need is for everyone to stop arguing with me."

"Sandor says you need these arrangements." Paulo strolled into the room to stand beside the bed and grin down at her. "Now, why are you being so difficult? Sandor has entrusted me with this mission, and you know I never fail at anything I undertake."

"This may be the exception to prove the rule. Since when have you accepted such unexciting assignments, Paulo?"

"I decided I owed it to Sandor. I didn't take as good care of his woman as I might have."

"Because I was shot? That wasn't anyone's fault but my own. It was my decision to go alone. You wanted to come with me."

Paulo shook his head. "Not because you were shot." His gaze was reproachful. "You didn't tell me about your feet. If you'd complained, I would have found a way to help you on our trip from the airfield. Sandor was very angry I had let you walk that distance."

"*Let?*"

He chuckled, and inclined his head in a half bow. "My apologies. Just then you sounded like my sister, Marna. I'm not fool enough to think a woman can't equal a man, but any person has to be taken care of when she or he is hurt." His smile vanished. "Now, let us be sensible. Sandor has many claims on his time right now. You may have slept for the last thirty-six hours, but he has not. I don't think he's snatched more than a few hours since the assault on Belajo began. He's very tired. He's been dividing his time between watching over you and establishing his government. If you insist on getting up, I'll have to tell him, and he will break off his meeting to come and argue with you, which means he will have to go back to the meeting later instead of resting. Do you want that?"

She frowned. "No, of course not."

"Then why not stay quietly in bed this afternoon and let him make his arrangements? In a few hours I will send a maid to help you with your bath and make you beautiful for him."

Dear heaven, she hadn't given a thought to how she looked. Even at her best, she was no beauty, and she was definitely not at her best now. She probably appeared as worn and frazzled as an old army boot. "I suppose I'm not very presentable."

Neither James nor Paulo answered, but their silence spoke volumes.

"Oh, very well." She sighed. "When are these 'arrangements' supposed to be set?"

"This evening. Sandor said he would be pleased if you would dine with him in the grand ballroom."

"The grand ballroom?" she repeated. "Are you sure that's what he said?"

Paulo nodded.

"Is it a party?"

Paulo shrugged. "He didn't say. I don't think so. He wouldn't want to tire you." He turned to leave. "I will go and arrange for the maid." He glanced pointedly at James. "It would be best if she rested now."

James rose hurriedly to his feet. "Yes, of course. I'll come to see you later, Alessandra." He followed Paulo to the door and paused to glance back and smile at her. "I doubt if I'm invited to your party. I have an idea Karpathan has a very private affair in mind this evening." He closed the door quietly behind him.

She hoped it was private. The only person she

wanted to see tonight was Sandor. But the grand ballroom? Perhaps it was some belated victory celebration. She slowly settled back in the bed and tried to relax. It wasn't easy. She wanted to see Sandor, touch him, talk to him. She was feeling terribly isolated. They had grown so close in their time together, she hadn't realized how lonely she would be when separated from him. Unfortunately, everyone in Tamrovia seemed to feel the same way.

And she didn't want to be alone now. She didn't want to have to think of that moment when she'd had to pull the trigger and seen Naldona fall to the floor. It had been too horrible to accept. But she had to accept it. She had taken a life. If she hadn't taken that life, others would have died. Still, she wished with all her heart that she hadn't been the one to have to do it. She closed her eyes. Perhaps it was better she had this time alone Since she had awakened, she had flinched away from thinking of what she had done. Now she had to face it and come to terms with it. She had faced many ugly shadows in her life, and this might be the ugliest one of all. Nevertheless, the shadow had to be confronted. She would lie here and try to nerve herself to confront what she had done.

The small, dark-skinned maid, who arrived in her suite a few hours later and identified herself as Bette, had obviously been given very explicit instructions. Alessandra was helped carefully into the bathroom, where she was bathed and her hair was shampooed and dried. Then she was wrapped in a bath sheet, transferred to the Queen Anne chair in the bedroom, and was manicured and pedicured. Her hair was curled and then brushed out to fall down her back in a shimmering flow of rich brown silk. Ordinarily, Bette's solemn determination to turn her into a pampered beauty would have amused and then exasperated Alessandra. However, she was still sore and weak enough to sit back and enjoy the cosseting.

"Makeup," Bette announced firmly. When it had been duly applied, the maid stood back and observed her critically. "Now you are beautiful."

"Not unless you're a sorceress," Alessandra said dryly. "There's only so much soap and paint can do. It's almost seven. I guess I might as well dress. The white gown will be fine."

"No, the Tanzar will send you what he wishes you to wear. You sit back and rest."

Sandor's "arrangements" covered attire as well, it seemed.

The gown was delivered ten minutes later. When Bette returned from answering the door, she was carefully carrying a garment that was a splash of magnificent color and fabric. The jade green of the brocade shimmered in the lamplight as if it were alive.

"Beautiful," Alessandra whispered. "I've never seen a gown so beautiful."

But she found it wasn't a gown at all. The garment proved to be a robe, full and flowing, with a high mandarin collar and wide sleeves. The robe itself was gloriously extravagant, and she felt absolutely royal as she slipped it on. Royal and confident and . . . treasured. She was still gazing bemusedly at herself in the mirror when another knock sounded. Paulo.

She turned to face him. "I feel as if I've been groomed to be the concubine of Kubla Khan."

"It's funny you should say that." Paulo's eyes were dancing. "You must have the power to see what others do not. My sister has such a power. Come, it's time." He scooped her up in his arms. "Now, do not protest. Sandor said you must not walk." He nodded to the maid to open the door. "I promise I will carry you only until we get to the foyer."

The reason for Paulo's amusement was at the bottom of the stairs, sitting squarely in the huge foyer.

"A ricksha." Alessandra couldn't believe it. Not just an ordinary ricksha, but a vehicle as extravagant as the robe she was wearing. The edge of the seat and the back of the ricksha were garlanded with gardenias and tuberoses, the wheels spoked with gold and studded with jade and amber. Standing beside it was a tall, powerful man in a scarlet uniform with gold braid. "But how did Sandor do it? There wasn't enough time."

"Everyone in Tamrovia is crazy to please Sandor. He only had to ask." Paulo sat her on the seat of the ricksha and motioned to the majordomo. One finger touched her cheek affectionately. "Joy." He stepped back.

The wheels of the ricksha had rubber rims, and the vehicle moved silently through the foyer and down the halls. Alessandra passed several soldiers standing at attention who were trying with some difficulty to repress their smiles. She didn't blame them. This entire scenario was completely outrageous. She didn't know whether to be more amused or touched.

The tall double doors were thrown open, and she caught her breath. Flowers were everywhere. White roses, jasmine, lilac. The scents were heady and fresh and the colors vibrant with a beauty that was a drug to the senses. The teardrop crystals of the huge chandelier reflected their hues like icicles in sunlight. Then she saw Sandor standing totally alone in the middle of the flower-bedecked ballroom and forgot everything but him. He was wearing a dark blue dress uniform embellished with only a narrow scarlet stripe down the sides of the trousers. No medals. No braid. Just Sandor.

The majordomo stopped before Sandor and, with a little flourish, set the arms of the ricksha on the floor and stood at attention.

"Sandor, are you trying to overwhelm me?" Alessandra asked with a shaky smile. "All of this . . ." She waved a hand. "I feel like someone in a fable."

"You're the type of woman men write fables about." He stepped closer and lifted her into his arms. "I've given you enough sordid reality to last you a lifetime. I wanted to give you something beautiful, for a change."

He had already given her something beautiful that had nothing to do with gold or jade or expensive brocade. Didn't he realize that? She opened her lips to ask him and then closed them again without speaking. Lord, he looked tired. Now that she was closer, she could see the shadows beneath his eyes and the deep grooves around his mouth. "Paulo said you hadn't been sleeping enough."

"I'll sleep later. There's too much to do right now."

"Including 'arranging' all this for me," she said in helpless exasperation. "I'll bet you haven't had a decent night's sleep for days, and yet you—"

"Hush." He set her down in the midst of a pile of satin pillows on a low, wide couch vaguely resembling a sultan's divan. "That wasn't work; it was pleasure." He brushed her lips lightly with his own. "*You're* a pleasure." He gestured and the majordomo left the room. "How are you?"

"Fine. Stiff, but better than you."

"Don't you ever give up?" He sat down beside her. "I'm a little tired, that's all." He suddenly frowned. "I know this is all a little glitzy, but I thought you might enjoy it."

She experienced a surge of love so great, she couldn't speak for a moment. He had planned this wonderful, thoughtful gesture and she hadn't even told him how much it meant to her. "I love it," she said softly. "It's utterly insane and completely glorious. Thank you, Sandor."

"You're welcome." He inclined his head, his frown disappearing. "I'm glad you appreciate it. You know, of course, I'm going to have to produce receipts for the new treasury department to prove I paid for it all out of my personal fortune. We mustn't have any hint of corruption in the government."

"You're definitely going to be the new president?"

"For one term, at least. We can't persuade anyone to run against me, so it looks as though I have no choice."

"You'll make a wonderful president."

"Will I?" He smiled crookedly. "'I don't know about that. I know how politics are played, but I've grown accustomed to bypassing diplomacy. Perhaps I'd better have someone around to keep an eye on me to make sure I don't become a dictator." He paused. "The job's open, Alessandra. All you have to do is apply."

"Watchdog?" She shook her head. "You wouldn't need me. There's no way on earth you could ever turn into another Naldona."

"The hell I don't need you." He knelt beside her, his eyes intent. "I'll always need you. Look, I know you're probably upset with me because of what happened to Naldona but—"

"Why should I be upset with you?" She stared at him in surprise. "It was my decision. You and Paulo seem to be on the same wavelength. No one is responsible for what I choose to do but me." She smiled sadly. "I know we made a deal, but there are some responsibilities we have to shoulder alone."

"I didn't want you to go through that." His voice was husky. "Why the hell didn't you go to Switzerland?"

"Because you were on your way to Belajo. Why the hell didn't you take me with you?"

"I wanted to keep you safe. This wasn't your war."

"But you were my man." Damn, she hadn't meant to say that. She moistened her lower lip with her tongue. "Weren't you? I've been called your woman so many times since the night we met, I've learned to accept it. But it has to go both ways."

"Yes, it has to go both ways." A smile tugged at

his lips. "But you should rephrase it to reflect the present tense. I *am* your man. Or perhaps the future tense is even a better idea. I will be your man." He paused. "Forever."

Joy, warmth, radiance. "I think I'll have to practice that for a while," she whispered. "I'm not used to thinking about forever."

"Neither am I. It's been a long time since I've dared to think more than one day at a time. But I want to get used to it, and I want to get used to it with you." He looked away, "Oh, hell, I'm rushing you again, aren't I? I didn't mean to pressure you into . . ." He made a motion to stand. "I'll tell them we're ready for dinner."

"No." Her hand on his sleeve prevented him from rising. "Not yet. I've been waiting all day to talk to you, and I have no intention of observing the social amenities until we have a few things clear."

He frowned. "I would have come to you the minute they told me you were awake, but—"

"I know. Paulo told me how busy you are. I'm not complaining of neglect. This time it was my place to come to you." She smiled. "Just as there will be times when it will be your place to come to me. We'll both have to learn to compromise."

He went still. "Does that mean you're going to stay with me?"

"Of course I'm going to stay. I would think you'd know that. I must have walked fifty miles for you in the last few days. I wouldn't do that for a man I was merely going to have dinner with"—she glanced around the lavishly decorated room—"though a dinner in a setting like this might have been very tempting."

"Why?" His tone was low and urgent. "Why are you going to stay with me?"

"I love you." Her smile faded, and she glared at him with sudden fierceness. "And you'd better love me too. I know I'm not as glamorous as some of the other women you've—"

His lips were on her own, cutting off the words. He raised his head. "Lord, yes, I love you." His eyes were glittering as they gazed down at her. "I was so damn scared I'd turned you off by all this violence and . . ." He kissed her again with joyous exuberance. "Of course I love you. Who'd be crazy enough to want glamour when he could have a fierce Amazon like you?"

"I can imagine there are a few men who suffer from that particular insanity," she said dryly. She was silent for a moment, searching for words. "I *am* fierce sometimes, and I have a lot of rough edges. That may come to annoy you. We're different people from different backgrounds." She made a face. "Which brings up the question of children. I want your children very much. Will you want to give them to a woman who has no knowledge of her parentage?"

He lowered his head to press his lips to the pulse throbbing in the hollow of her throat. "I thought we'd agreed I was to share my background with you." His gaze lifted to meet her eyes. "Bloodlines are just nonsense. You have strength, intelligence, courage, and honesty. I'll be damn lucky if I can offer as much to our child." His eyes began to twinkle. "And I'll be glad to initiate the procedure of impregnating you immediately, if it will offer you any reassurance. We can always hold dinner."

She experienced a hot, clenching sensation in the pit of her stomach. It had been too long since their night together. All she had to do was nod, and . . .

But he was exhausted, and he had probably been skipping meals as well as sleep. "Later." She buried her face in his shoulder, and her words were muffled. "I *want* to be gentle. I want to give you gentleness and love and everything you need from me. I'll try so hard. I want you to know that."

"Gentleness is something we'll both have to work on." His hand was tenderly stroking the back of her head. "I'm a little out of practice myself."

"I can't give up my work. It's too important to me."

"I wouldn't want you to give it up. I'll give you carte blanche here in Tamrovia. If you feel you have to visit any other country, I'll try to arrange to go with you."

"That may be difficult for you to do as president of Tamrovia."

His chuckle reverberated beneath her ear. "Has it occurred to you that you may have the same difficulty? You won't be the Tanzar's woman then. You'll be the president's first lady." His laughter broke off abruptly. "You will marry me, won't you? I know you don't like the idea of becoming involved in politics, but—"

"I'll marry you." She lifted her head to look up at him and smile. "Perhaps it's time I stopped criticizing and started doing. I have to warn you, though, I have a tendency to throw myself into projects with a good deal of enthusiasm. You may wish you hadn't asked me."

"No, I'll never wish that." He kissed her lightly, lovingly. "This choice is one I'll never regret."

Choices again. They had both had to make so many painful ones in the past. Now they could hope for better alternatives from which to choose. Joy and love and freedom. Wonderful choices.

And responsibility. She was feeling the weight of that responsibility now as she looked at Sandor. He was so very tired, but she knew he wouldn't rest. He had planned this evening for her and wouldn't willingly relinquish his gift. Well, obviously there was only one thing to do.

She feigned a yawn and gazed up at him with eyes that were clear and innocent. "Now that we've settled a few of our problems, do you suppose I could lie down for a few minutes before dinner? I feel a little weak."

Sandor frowned in concern. "Perhaps you shouldn't have gotten up tonight. Would you like me to take you back to your room?"

"No, I'll be fine. Just give me a few minutes to rest." She leaned back on the silk pillows of the divan, pulling him down to lie beside her. "Hold me."

"You're sure?" His arms slid around her and held her close to the warm hardness of his body.

"Very sure." She shifted his head to rest on her shoulder and began gently to stroke his hair. "I want to be close to you. I like this, don't you?"

"Yes." His eyes were already closing. "So sweet . . ." His lips nuzzled the side of her throat. "Tell me when you feel rested enough to have dinner, love."

"I will."

He was deeply asleep in minutes. Alessandra's hand continued to stroke his hair. She had never realized she could feel this poignant tenderness. Perhaps she was actually learning gentleness. Yet the tenderness was still interwoven with fierce protectiveness. Maybe the two qualities could exist side by side. She hoped so. Sandor would need her fierceness as well as her gentleness in the future. He was a man who would always neglect his own welfare in order to give more than he should. She would have to guard him well. And she would start tonight.

She would see that he wasn't disturbed and slept the whole night through. Eating could wait. Passion could wait. If any of his blasted cabinet members decided they couldn't do without Sandor, they'd have to wait too. She brushed her lips lingeringly over his forehead. And if those gentlemen gave her any arguments, they'd learn just how fierce the Tanzar's woman could be when she was protecting the man she loved.

THE EDITOR'S CORNER

"Jolly" and "heartwarming" are words I don't hear or see nearly enough these days. That's a pity because they're wonderful words ... as well as the perfect ones to describe the quartet of romances we're publishing next month to start off the New Year with warmth and cheer.

In **DISTURBING THE PEACE,** LOVESWEPT #178, Peggy Webb gives us a worthy successor to her intense, yet madcap romance **DUPLICITY,** LOVESWEPT #157. This book is particularly well-titled because heroine Amy Logan, an inventor, truly does disturb the peace of her new neighbor Judge Todd Cunningham. Amy has a few problems perfecting her creations— like an erratic robot named Herman and a musical bed that isn't correctly programed to observe the fine distinctions between night and day. Todd is lovestruck from their first meeting, and Amy is clearly captivated by the sexy judge ... but she is also terrified of the risk he represents. Mistakenly interpreting Amy's resistance to her miscasting of him as a stuffy legal-beagle, Todd sets out to change her image of him. With a bit of assistance from Amy's zany mystery writer aunt and lots of virile charm on his own part, Todd merrily campaigns to win over the imp who has stolen his heart. A sheer delight.

Joan Elliott Pickart really outdoes herself with her next love story, **KALEIDOSCOPE,** LOVESWEPT #179. And in the secondary characters in this book, she creates two of the most delightful ladies it's been my pleasure to meet in a long, long time. Those "ladies" are devoted to liberating themselves from conventional expectations for "older people." They are also the loving mothers of our heroine and hero. Now, when these two formidable matchmaking moms plot to get their offspring introduced to each other, they do

(continued)

so in a fashion that sets the kaleidoscope of life swirling with brilliant color. Heroine Mallory Carson is a beauty and hero Michael Patterson is one gorgeous blond hunk of a divorce lawyer. Naturally Michael has seen enough of the miserable side of married life to be turned off even to the words "happily ever after," much less to believe in them. Still, he can't resist Mallory and is even drawn to her day care center, a spot he would find a most awkward one for him if Mallory was not there. Then, when the rainbow colors of love explode before the very eyes of this pair who consider themselves mismatched, they have to take the biggest chance of all.

Don't miss this wonderfully humorous and emotionally moving love story.

Patt Bucheister gives us just what every woman needs in LOVESWEPT #180, **THE DRAGON SLAYER**. She gives us a white knight in Webb Hunter. When Webb falls—literally—on and for our heroine Abigail Stout he soon decides to appoint himself her own special slayer of dragons, bringing her teddy bears and toys . . . and his promise of earth shattering passion. Abigail has been to busy with school and work and more work to have had much experience with men, so she is ill-prepared for the pursuit of Webb, who is as enchanted by her saucy personality and her beauty as he is by her most intriguing perfume: vanilla extract! Abby has learned the hard way (shunted from one foster family to another during her childhood) that happiness is fleeting and dreams do not come true . . . and she is as hard pressed to resist Webb as she is to believe in his promises. Just as you responded to Patt's first LOVESWEPT (**NIGHT AND DAY,** #130) so, too, I think, you will respond with enormous enthusiasm for this touching and memorable romance.

Is there any writer more evocative or imaginative than Fayrene Preston? Her zany cast of characters in
(continued)

ROBIN AND HER MERRY PEOPLE, LOVESWEPT #181, will worm their way into your affections just as they do hero Jarrod Saxon's. Heroine Gena Alexander has run from Jarrod whom she is convinced has betrayed her love, her trust. Starting a new life with her merry (but poor) people, Gena's eyes are opened to human suffering and to tragedy, and, like Robin Hood, she determines to do something about them. When Jarrod tracks her down and makes his intentions clear, both are jolted into an awareness of dimensions of each other that are different from any they'd ever even guessed existed. Discovery . . . joy . . . and complications because of the merry band's problems lead to Jarrod's and Gena's deep and rich revelations about the true meaning of love. This is throbbingly sensual and utterly charming romance that we believe you will long remember.

Chuckles and surprises, passion and affection abound to make for *jolly* and *heartwarming* LOVE-SWEPT reading next month. Enjoy!

Warm regards,

Sincerely,

Carolyn Nichols

Carolyn Nichols
   Editor
LOVESWEPT
Bantam Books, Inc.
666 Fifth Avenue
New York, NY 10103

Heirs to a great dynasty, the Delaney brothers were united by blood, united by devotion to their rugged land . . . and known far and wide as

THE SHAMROCK TRINITY

Bantam's bestselling LOVESWEPT romance line built its reputation on quality and innovation. Now, a remarkable and unique event in romance publishing comes from the same source: THE SHAMROCK TRINITY, three daringly original novels written by three of the most successful women's romance writers today. Kay Hooper, Iris Johansen, and Fayrene Preston have created a trio of books that are dynamite love stories bursting with strong, fascinating male and female characters, deeply sensual love scenes, the humor for which LOVESWEPT is famous, and a deliciously fresh approach to romance writing.

THE SHAMROCK TRINITY—Burke, York, and Rafe: Powerful men . . . rakes and charmers . . . they needed only love to make their lives complete.

☐ RAFE, THE MAVERICK by Kay Hooper

Rafe Delaney was a heartbreaker whose ebony eyes held laughing devils and whose lilting voice could charm any lady—or any horse—until a stallion named Diablo left him in the dust. It took Maggie O'Riley to work her magic on the impossible horse . . . and on his bold owner. Maggie's grace and strength made Rafe yearn to share the raw beauty of his land with her, to teach her the exquisite pleasure of yielding to the heat inside her. Maggie was stirred by Rafe's passion, but would his reputation and her ambition keep their kindred spirits apart?   (21786 • $2.50)

 LOVESWEPT

☐ YORK, THE RENEGADE by Iris Johansen

Some men were made to fight dragons, Sierra Smith thought when she first met York Delaney. The rebel brother had roamed the world for years before calling the rough mining town of Hell's Bluff home. Now, the spirited young woman who'd penetrated this renegade's paradise had awakened a savage and tender possessiveness in York: something he never expected to find in himself. Sierra had known loneliness and isolation too—enough to realize that York's restlessness had only to do with finding a place to belong. Could she convince him that love was such a place, that the refuge he'd always sought was in her arms?

(21787 • $2.50)

☐ BURKE, THE KINGPIN by Fayrene Preston

Cara Winston appeared as a fantasy, racing on horseback to catch the day's last light—her silver hair glistening, her dress the color of the Arizona sunset . . . and Burke Delaney wanted her. She was on his horse, on his land: she would have to belong to him too. But Cara was quicksilver, impossible to hold, a wild creature whose scent was midnight flowers and sweet grass. Burke had always taken what he wanted, by willing it or fighting for it; Cara cherished her freedom and refused to believe his love would last. Could he make her see he'd captured her to have and hold forever?

(21788 • $2.50)